The Best Campfire Stories

The Best Campfire Stories

A Collection of Chilling Campfire Tales to Spook, Thrill and Freak You Out in the Woods!

An Outdoors Club Publication

An Outdoors Club Publication

COVER ILLUSTRATION BY NICO PHOTOS

INTERIOR ILLUSTRATIONS BY ELIZABETH SULLIVAN

COVER DESIGN & LAYOUT BY MICHAEL GRAFFAM

INTERIOR DESIGN BY KELLY RENO

EDITORIAL STAFF; Bob Sullivan, Kat Martell, Kelly Reno, Lucy Quigley, Sue Zenger and Joanna Celeste.

Summary: An original collection of short and spooky campfire tales.

ISBN 978-9796379-95 (trade paper)
1. Campfire Stories. 2. Ghost Stories 3. Outdoor Tales

Published by The Way to Happiness Outdoors Club
10915 Deliban Avenue, Tujunga, CA 91042
www.TWTHOC.org

Contents

Introduction

The Way to Happiness Outdoors Club is a group of dedicated volunteers that organizes family outdoor sporting activities to raise funds to print and distribute the booklet, *The Way to Happiness®*, a common sense guide to making good choices in life.

Being an outdoors club, we've heard plenty of spooky campfire stories over the years and decided to put together this collection of original tales. In this book you'll find some of our favorite campfire stories including true stories that actually happened, tall tales that never happened and stories that fall somewhere in between. Because all of the stories in this book are new and original, you probably haven't heard them before which makes reading them for the first time all the more fun.

As you sit around the campfire with your friends or nestled in your sleeping bag with a flashlight reading this book, we hope it sends chills down your spine or even makes you laugh out loud.

But beware of the werewolves, aliens, ghosts and mad men that just might leap out of the pages! And if you hear strange footsteps outside your tent or something howling off in the distance, don't get too freaked out. They're just stories—aren't they?

The Editors

* As a favor to the parents out there, we've included story ratings in our table of contents to avoid frightening very young children. Stories marked, "SCARY!" are not for young kids, stories marked, "ALL AGES" are suitable for general audiences and stories marked, "KIDS" are suitable for young children in our opinion. Regardless, we suggest that you read the stories first before retelling them to the kids because you know your children better than anyone. Happy reading!

Because It Tastes Good

By Dick Sullivan

Voted the #1 Best Campfire Story

IT'S MY TURN TO TELL A STORY?

These woods have been so cold lately, so first let me thank you for letting a stranger warm his bones at your campfire. It always surprises me that the young… *peopl*e… are so… nice.

Let's see. A story. Well, I guess I ought to tell you this one particular tale, because frankly, if there are any others like me here, none of *them* are likely to give you any warning.

And, you see, my story *is* a warning.

It was a late autumn day and our Georgia sun was gone behind the ridge, turning the clouds over Haystack Mountain blood red. I was done fishing my secret stream, hurrying along so I wouldn't miss Ma's hot biscuit dinner, when I was surprised to meet Jack Splint coming down an old logging trail. It wasn't usual to see Jack away from home this time of day, not when his pa could be working him at chores around their place up on No-Name Mountain. A ragged old cane pole swung from his hand, and I figured he'd been out fishing his private spots along the river, too. Neither of us was carrying any fish, so there wasn't any need to ask if the trout was biting.

"'Lo, Jack," I said. "See you got out for a spell."

"Carter Johnson's bein' et by vampires and wildwolves," Jack said right off, "and it won't be long before he joins up with 'em in the woods."

Now I didn't want to be talking about vampires and wildwolves out on the river road with night coming on and a good hike home still to go, so I said, "Jack, I swear. You ought to stop with such tales. There's no wildwolves or vampires in the woods and there's no witches and no rock demons nor any other kind of boogiebear. Look at you. A day of fishin' and no chores, and you got to talk all *spooky*."

But Jack went right on, "Them wild things are out in the woods at night, all right, now it's gettin' on to Hallow's Eve. And they're eatin' on Carter Johnson; pretty soon he's gonna turn into one himself. I know because the new girl told me, and *she* can talk to animals."

And so it was I first learned about Emily from arguing with Jack Splint, the saddest-looking fellow you ever saw, a year older than me and tall and skinny and living a hard life with a drunken pa and a little mouse of a ma, who looked about as sad as Jack did. Jack seemed even gloomier now than usual, looking all around him kind of hollow-cheeked and wild-eyed.

"Why, I guess I'll go to school tomorrow," I said, meaning the one-room shack rented to the county by old man Elliot and run by our schoolmarm, Miss Paltry. "I didn't know we had any new girls. Is she pretty?"

"She's a peach," Jack said. "But she ain't in school yet. Her family's moved up to the old Pilgrim Sr. farm, and there's too much work, I guess."

Jack went on about the new girl, living up on Haystack Mountain, north side, where the Frank Pilgrim Sr. farm burnt down years ago, leaving only the stables and some beat-up old sheds. It was a terrible affair. The family lost some children in the fire and in their grief moved away. The farm had been deserted ever since. Jack was out in the overgrown fields hunting anything useful when Emily appeared out of nowhere and startled him silly. He dropped the arrowheads and broken plow blade he'd found right away.

"She was friendly and asked me up to dinner," Jack went on, "but I had to get home, else Pa would lay on me with the switch if I was late. Before I could go, a squirrel came running by and stopped at her feet. That little squirrel commenced kinda twitchin' and squeakin' at her and durn if she wasn't squeakin' right back at it before it tore off again. 'That little squirrel's afraid of the vampires and wildwolves,' she said. 'Same as Carter Johnson, 'cause every night they come to his house and call him outside, and bite him and drink his blood. Pretty soon, he'll be a wildwolf himself. Oh, come up and have dinner with us. We're having lamb, and it tastes *so* good.' But

Pa's hickory switch don't taste so good and I couldn't be late and I ran on home. That was Saturday night a week ago. I saw Carter Johnson at school after that and he was a strange one, ever' single day. He's bein' et by wildwolves, and that's a fact."

That was the most talk I ever heard from Jack Splint at one time. I hadn't been to school in a week, since Pa didn't make me go if I wanted to do chores for Ma and fish instead. And so I hadn't seen Carter Johnson lately with my own eyes, but I didn't believe such nonsense anyway. I was, however, very curious about the new girl.

"Who'd buy that old farm?" I asked. "The house is burnt down to the rock walls and there's nothin' left but old broke-down horse stables."

Jack shrugged. "I can't be late, got to be goin'. Stay out of them woods and stay away from Carter Johnson because them vampires are eatin' him up."

Before I could argue with Jack any more, the road humped over a small plank bridge and divided. Jack waved goodbye and headed for the trail that led up to No-Name Mountain and his pa's stinky old shack. I often wished better for poor Jack Splint, but by the time I'd followed the fork up to the county road, I was thinking only about the new girl and how she could talk to the animals. It was a skill I had dearly longed to discover in myself, but the coons and spring fawns and squirrels and chipmunks and such that I chanced upon or stalked in the woods only responded to my words and outstretched fingers by making hasty departures. After so much rude treatment I had bid farewell to my dream of talking to the beasts of the forest. Here, though, was someone who might have the gift! Jack was a truthful boy, gloomy or not; he had seen her talk to the squirrel. Maybe I could learn animal-talking after all, if she would teach me.

I hurried my feet along, trying not to think about the predicament little Carter Johnson might be in, my eyes full of the glorious red sky. As a young boy I always loved the mountains in the fall, even when it was getting dark around me and nonsense talk about vampires and wildwolves got my goosebumps up. Though it was years and years ago, and though I never really got a chance to grow old myself, I think of those golden autumn afternoons and starry velvet nights the way an old man might look back fondly on a pleasant childhood, which up to that time I mostly had. Summers were hot and winters were cold, but in between there was fall, and fall suited me fine. I lived up in the north Georgia mountains, in Odala County, with Pa and Ma and old PawPaw, my pa's daddy, who lost an ear and one of his legs in the Yankee war. PawPaw was handy with crafting things: he made a wooden leg for himself and when he strapped it on he could do most things any other carpenter could do on two natural ones. We all lived in a big one-room cabin Pa and PawPaw built, and for most of my life from the time I could walk until I was nine years old, which is when I met Emily, I did chores for Ma and kept the firewood stacked up and went to school and fished. I had secret spots for fishing and kept Ma busy even in winter cooking up skinny little brook trout and wily bluemouth catfish—they tasted so *good*! We were a happy family, and I thought life would go on like that forever, a life of seasons spent in changing weather, fall being my favorite, but then I met Emily and learned that life, just like the weather, had seasons too.

When I finally got home that night, it was dark and the crickets were quieting down early now that cooler weather was falling. Ma gave me a big hug and scolded me for being out so late, then sat me down by the fireplace for biscuits she'd kept warmed. So delicious! They tasted good, too! I had them with berry jam and scrambled eggs, which it was our custom to eat at night, meat being scarce on occasion. Pa and PawPaw sat beneath the oil lantern and locked wits over the chess game PawPaw had carved up and given Pa and me for Christmas one year. Ma got out her guitar and sang ballads so pretty that I saw

PawPaw, bad hearing and all, wiping the corners of his eyes. Before long I was asleep beside her, and Pa picked me up and laid me up in my loft, where he and Ma kissed me goodnight before retiring to the far side of the cabin and pulling the curtains on their own cherry-wood bed. Outside, the darkness dashed itself against mountains and streams and little feet scurried along rock walls and in deep brush. Vampires and wildwolves might be roaming, but the warmth and life of our little cabin was a fortress. I rolled onto my side and the last thing I saw before sleep overcame me was PawPaw settling into the old rocker, pulling on his spectacles and opening up the Good Book to read himself into the night, as he always did. And as it always did, too, there against the wall beside him leaned his big, long-barrel shotgun, as though maybe in some way known only to PawPaw, his long-ago war wasn't over yet, and the coming of night meant going on guard, not to sleep.

Next day I was up early, helping Ma with breakfast. Pa left to do his lumberman's work and I put on my school clothes and ran most of the way to school.

"Well, look who's here," Miss Paltry said, as I passed into the schoolhouse.

My curiosity was up and I planned to study Carter Johnson and talk to Jack Splint some more, but Jack didn't come to school that day and Carter Johnson couldn't have seemed more like himself. In fact, it was all the *other* children who seemed sort of odd, not talking much or horsing around as was the usual state of affairs. They seemed drained or something, pale and unsmiling, and for the most part ignored me. Carter was a year younger than me, a head shorter, and a kind sort of soul, easy to make a joke on and easy to regret teasing for the way it could hurt his feelings. After English and morning arithmetic, Miss Paltry gave her normally rowdy class of Georgia farm children an early recess for behaving so well. Carter and I left the solemn crowd of children and raced over to the oak tree with the hanging ropes and took turns seeing who could leap the farthest. I beat him easily and he took it good-naturedly, the way he always did. Then we plopped down on our backs and chewed long-stemmed weedgrass, looking up at a cloudless sky scribbled on by a formation of ducks beating their way down to Florida. A couple of specks floated alongside, keeping up.

"Them's hawks," Carter said. "Looking for stragglers. A duck gets behind and one of them hawks will get him." He was quiet a moment. "The natural world don't take no mercy on the innocent, that's what Pa says." He looked over at me. "Think of poor Jack Splint. It's like the world is a wolf, eatin' him a little bit at a time. I do wish his pa would just up and drown in a river, I do, for the way he treats him."

"Why, hard words, Carter," I said.

"I reckon. But Jack's a decent fellow and doesn't ever'one deserve a chance at a good life? I don't think Jack's got a mean bone in him and look at how he gets used."

"I guess life ain't always fair," I had to agree. I never heard such deep thoughts before.

"It's on us to be right to each other," Carter went on, moving his face close to mine. "Each other is all we've got. You and me can be good to old Jack Splint. That's better'n wishin' his mean pa a drownin', now I think of it."

Carter turned sunny again. He gave me a punch on the arm and laughed. I sat up and gave him a shove as Miss Paltry began ringing the class bell.

"Race you," Carter said and took off. I gave him a bit of a lead and then caught him easily. We pulled up in line still laughing and pushing, sidling in with the quiet, brooding bunch of farm children who mostly stared at the ground.

"Settle down, you two, and file in all of you like you'll be ladies and gentlemen one of these days," Miss Paltry said. Her hair bun was pulled up so tight I think it stretched her jaw and made it hard to talk. But we did as commanded and I struggled through history lessons, science and afternoon arithmetic, until four o'clock finally came. At the first syllable of "Class dismissed," I was out the door and flying up toward River Road. It was uphill, but I hurried along, driven by an excitement that had stirred on first hearing from Jack Splint about the new girl. A girl who could talk to animals! Someone who had the secret!

I got a stitch in my side soon enough and had to slow down, but at River Road Fork the trail began dropping and I took to running again, over the humped bridge and past the logging trail where I had met Jack Splint the day before. The trail widened and gave onto River Road and I bore myself onward, paying no attention to the darkness gathering in the wild shrubs along the road or to the deepening of the skies glimpsed through mingled leaves of oak, chalk maple, cottonwood and pine. I ran for all I was worth and before I knew it, I pulled up where a broad but untended trail left the main road. The top of Haystack Mountain burned red in the sunset; pockets of shadow formed a hundred caves in the green and black woods below. In one of these dark holes I could just make out the ruined stables on the Frank Pilgrim Sr. farm. It wasn't far now and I left River Road and set off down the trail at a walk, to get my breath back. In a few minutes more I turned onto a cart track and was past the tumbledown gate of the farm and stood looking up at the remains of the farm itself.

The fire that drove the Pilgrim Sr. family from our mountain left only the blackened stone walls of the foundation. From the top of the foundation I looked down into the basement, at charred and twisted timbers scattered and floating in a dark pool of rainwater and moss. Above me the sun was gone beyond the mountains and in the purple patch of the sky's ceiling, stars were just beginning to sprout.

"Hello!" I shouted.

Beyond the farmhouse pit were the stables, only partly burned but with their roofs half-caved in and their doors off their hinges and lying broken on the ground. I walked over and looked inside the nearest stable. The stalls were empty and leaning, but in the back there was a child's bed all neatly made up in white linen. Above the bed a constellation of little figurines hung from a wire frame covered in the same cloth. The figurines appeared to be of school-age children; books and ponytails and fishing poles hung from hands and heads. At their center, not suspended but lying on a fold of white blanket, was a curious figure. I couldn't tell what kind, but it looked like an animal, colored deep red. Its mouth was open, as if eating, and its eyes yellow below alert, peaked ears and a big bushy tail, that, as I stared at it, gave the illusion of being in motion.

Now I don't know why, but a shiver overtook me and I couldn't make myself go inside the stable proper. When I turned from the doorway, I nearly jumped into next week. There stood a little girl completely still, watching me like a hawk.

"Hello," she said, and a warm smile appeared on her face. She also was dressed in white, but dimmer, as though a small lantern burned inside her but had been turned down.

"Are you Emily?" I asked.

"I most certainly am, and I guess Jack Splint told you my pa bought this poor old farm."

"He did, for a fact," I said, "and that you're too busy with your new home to come to school yet."

"And did he tell you Pa won't be having any young ruffians picking through his fields any more?"

"I ain't a scavenger," I said, a little riled by such direct talk. "Jack told me you can talk to the animals."

Emily laughed. She certainly was pretty as a peach, all right. She had merry eyes and red cheeks, and hair bright as sunflowers curled in ringlets all the way down her back.

"What else did he tell you?" she asked, dancing a little where she stood.

"Well, not much, only that wildwolves and vampires are eatin' my friend Carter Johnson, and he's doomed to roam in the woods."

"That sounds like silly boy's talk. Who believes in vampires and wildwolves? Have you ever seen any?"

I hadn't, but before I could answer, she clapped her hands and said, "You should come up for dinner, up on the hill where we're staying while Pa builds us a house. You could meet Pa, and have tender young calf with us. Last week we had lamb. The young animals taste so *good*."

"But I can't stay," I said. "It's late and I'll have to run all the way home or Ma will be mad. But tell me, can you teach *me* how to talk to the animals?" I tried to keep from sounding as desperate as I felt.

Emily's eyes twinkled. "You come back tomorrow after school with Carter Johnson and Jack Splint, so I can box Jack's ears for telling tall tales." She leaned closer and added, "And I'll show you and Carter some secrets about the young animals. But only if you bring your friends."

"Why, all right," I said. "If I can coax them to come, I will. What kind of secrets?"

"See you tomorrow," Emily laughed. She turned and skipped away to what was a small trail leading up the hillside, where she paused to wave, and then was gone. The purple light of sunset moved right in to fill the hole where she'd stood.

Still standing in the stable's rough doorway, I looked back inside at the small bed against the far wall. Something was different. The figurines of children hung from their cloth-covered wires as before, but now they revolved around an empty bedspread. The odd little animal figure had vanished. Or had it really been there?

I had a long run home and I started out at a good gallop. It was mostly downhill and I was too excited to care about the night coming on or the owls screeching or even the far away roar of an angry black bear. Before I knew it I was past the old plank bridge and the river and tearing along the county road, only a mile from home, when I heard something pacing me in the woods alongside. Or I thought I did. I stopped and listened, breathing hard and heart pounding, scared but not really scared. The woods were quiet. And so I raced on home, cartwheeled over Pa's front gate and made it inside just as Ma was setting the table with more hot biscuits and eggs and a bowl of fresh tomatoes Pa had surprised her with from the general store down the mountain. It all tasted so *good*! I ate hearty and so did Pa and PawPaw and Ma hardly had any dishes to wash up, every plate was licked so clean. With a full belly and tired out from my long run, I slipped up into my loft early and let Ma's guitar sweep me away.

That night in the tiny hours something seemed to land on the roof of our cabin, waking me up from a dark, distant land. But our cabin was a fortress, and I only smiled and was rolling over to go back to sleep when I heard the back door slam open and PawPaw thumping along on the log floor with his wooden leg and yelling, "Git out, you demon!" and there was a flash that lit up the dark like lightning and then thunder from PawPaw's ten-gauge shotgun. From the back of the cabin Pa came charging up with his Navy Colt and the oil lantern. I jumped down from bed but Ma gathered me up and sat me down in her lap at the table, clutching me so tight I could hardly breathe. In a few minutes Pa and PawPaw came back inside, turned down the lantern and closed and bolted the door. They spoke quietly and then went around throwing the bars on the front door and the windows. Pa took Ma aside and PawPaw came and sat down at the table with me.

"Now after school tomorrow you come right back on home," he said. "Don't you be going fishing or visiting or lingering with girls or nary a thing else. It's back on home when that old maid Paltry closes her book and sets you free. Now you do as PawPaw says." He cocked his head and pointed his good ear at me. "Is it a promise?"

I hesitated only a heartbeat and said, "Yessir, like you said."

"Promise to keep?"

"Yessir."

"All right, then. Ever' once a while, the woods go bad. A few moons pass and them devils move on. 'Til then you stay close to your pa or his pa, and keep your promises. Now up with you and back to sleep, the night's good 'til morning."

PawPaw lifted me up and gave me a hug, tickling me with his white stubble beard. In his arms it was only natural for all alarm to drain from me and by the time he tucked me in I was drifting back into the same sweet sleep I had always known.

Morning came late through the closed windows; Pa was long gone to work. PawPaw was outside with a ladder on the roof and I rushed through breakfast with Ma so I could get to school on time. Racing away on the county road I waved to PawPaw up on the roof, but he was staring at something at his feet and didn't see me. Up the road into a beautiful fall day I went. Moths pretty as butterflies, that PawPaw called Cloudywings, flitted among the trees, with the morning sun lighting them and the autumn-yellow leaves from behind. In the treetops a woodpecker pecked and birds everywhere sang up a storm. Way up high in another perfect sky, long flimsy lines of wintering ducks rode the winds on down south to the swamplands. Impatience and excitement drove me onward, and in no time I was passing under the Eliot farm sign and running out back to the schoolhouse. The steps leading to the schoolhouse door were empty, no children anywhere. Up those steps and through the door I went, and there was Miss Paltry looking up sternly from her desk. Jack Splint sat in front of her to one side, and across from him Carter Johnson held a pencil and smiled at me as I drew up short in front of Miss Paltry. Jack and Carter were the only students in the room, and now there was me.

"Late as usual," Miss Paltry said. "But the devil gets his due, at least you did come. I guess I have never seen the likes of this, three of thirteen children appearing on a school day, and the rest of them missing the spelling bee. Take your seat. Open up your numbers book to page nineteen and work the exercises. I have a dozen letters to write to parents."

I sat down and did as I was told. Carter made a face and shrugged his shoulders. Jack Splint looked positively ill; his face was ash grey but he smiled shyly over at me before returning to his numbers. The morning's impatience rode over me like a horse now and it seemed forever until Miss Paltry finished her tattletale letters and got us through arithmetic and reading chores. But at last, she gave us a recess.

Carter and I dashed outside with Jack Splint following so slow I grew downright irritable. Beneath the oak tree with the swinging ropes I could finally spill out my excitement.

When I was done, Carter just said, "I shouldn't go if I'll be late home. Ma's got pumpkin pie tonight and when I'm late to table I don't get dessert."

"Why, we won't be late at all," I said. "If you and Jack come with me, she'll teach us both secret things and we'll be able to talk to the animals. Please do come! I promise we won't stay long and you won't be late."

"Promise to keep?" Carter said.

"Surely indeed," I said.

"I'll go," said Jack Splint. "She's a peach."

"Where is everybody?" I asked. "I never saw such a empty bunch of school desks."

"Miss Paltry's spelling bee scared 'em off," Jack Splint said, and giggled.

Miss Paltry rang the bell and we marched back into class. Lunchtime finally came and I had apples and cornbread and some dried ham Ma packed for me. Carter's ma sent him along cornbread and jerky and a tomato. Jack Splint didn't have a lunch pail and said he had no appetite that day.

"You look like food's what you need," Carter said. "Have this 'mato."

"Naw. Breakfast was fine," Jack said. "Big dinner last night, too." He lay down in the grass, closed his eyes and chewed on a long stem of weed.

Carter and I did some mumblety-peg and a swing challenge. For the first time I couldn't beat Carter in a long jump from the rope. It made me mad, but I tried not to show it.

"I been practicin' out in the yard," Carter explained. "Pa fixed up a rope on the maple tree and showed me how to let go at the right time."

"Durn if you didn't beat me by two feet," I said, and punched him on the arm. He punched me back and there was the bell again and back we ran to class. Miss Paltry cancelled the spelling bee. The afternoon was terrible slow, so slow I thought it would never end, but finally Miss Paltry took off her glasses and unwound her jaws and said, "This pitiful class is dismissed."

Carter and I were through the door at the same time and out to the road before Jack Splint came painfully down the stairs. In the afternoon sun he looked shriveled and worn.

"Y'all go on," he yelled and waved his hand. "Meet you there."

That was all we needed to hear. As fast as we could go Carter and I blazed along the county road, down the trail where it forked over the plank bridge and then up River Road, laughing and racing, too full of a bright fall day to slow down even a little bit. Even on the uphill climb from the river's edge we hardly lost a step; finally, though, we came to a halt, huffing and puffing, still laughing, hands on knees or shoving each other. After a while we straightened up, breathing regular, and found ourselves looking across a jumble of trees and brush at the ruins of the Pilgrim Sr. farm.

"Almost there," I said cheerfully. "Let's walk on up."

"Wonder what time it is," Carter said. "Seems the dark is comin' on fast."

I looked up and was surprised to find the skies turning toward evening. There was plenty of sunlight left, but it did seem later in the day than it should be.

"Why, it can't be half past four," I said. "We just left school and been runnin' since."

Carter was quiet a moment and then said, "Maybe Miss Paltry kept us late and didn't tell us."

"Now why would she do that? Here, let's run on over and get those secrets we came for."

But Carter said, "I don't want to be late home. I promised Ma."

"And I promised you, one to keep," I said, a bit annoyed. "I can't learn those secrets without you."

"If it gets much darker, I'm leaving. I promised."

"Let's run then, not stand here wastin' time."

I dashed off and that seemed to pull Carter behind me. Down the weedy trail and onto the farm track we ran, past the old fallen gate, pulling up at the blackened foundation. We stared into the murk of the basement.

"There's secrets down *there*," Carter said. "But I don't want to know 'em."

"Hello!" I shouted. Carter and I looked around. There was no reply.

"Well, where is she?" Carter asked.

"Probably coming down the hill now," I said. "Come look at this!" I ran over to the remains of the stable and peered inside. Even as my eyes adjusted it remained dark and formless. Carter poked his head beside me.

"What?" he said.

"Why, I swear," I answered. The gloom was all fuzzy and foggy; the stalls still leaned at crazy angles but at the back there was nothing: no child's bed, no white linens, no figurines in linen-covered wire. Through a gap in the stable planks I was startled to see, so soon after school ending, the twinkle of a distant star.

"*Hell-oo-ooo*," a voice came from behind us.

Carter and I turned around and took a few steps. There at the little trail Emily had used yesterday stood Jack Splint, beckoning us over.

"Up here a ways," he said, smiling. He looked even paler and skinnier if possible, wavering a bit side to side, making it look unnatural to stand on two legs. The last rays of the sun were slipping over Haystack Mountain behind him, turning the clouds redder than I had ever seen them. But somehow the clouds' reflection had lightened the woods and sky and given the day a look of afternoon again, as if the clock of the world had slipped its moorings.

"This way," Jack repeated.

"I don't want to be late," Carter said to me.

"We won't stay ten minutes," I replied. "Just long enough to get our secrets. Come on, let's find Emily."

"Ten minutes, no more," said Carter.

We ran over to catch up with Jack but Jack set off and surprisingly we could not catch him. He bounded easily up the trail, laughing now as he bounced along, staying the same distance ahead of us.

"Why, suddenly he's a *cham*peen runner," grumbled Carter and we both laughed. Jack bore us on steadily upward, where the trail finally leveled off. Carter came to a halt behind me, and I stopped, too.

"It must be nearly dinnertime," he said. "Look up there, will you?"

I did look overhead. The sky was all shades of red, a quilt of bloody dark swirls against lighter patches, like no sunset I had ever seen before. At the roof of the world a black pool of twilight spread downward like ink.

"Way up high," Carter said, pointing, but I had already seen the ducks V-formed and journeying southward. A lone speck trailed them, a straggler, and then from a dark red blot a larger form streaked and fell on the single duck. In a heartbeat the merged forms disappeared back into the bloody clot of cloud.

"Hawk," Carter said.

For just a moment I felt my heart sink. "Duck got careless," I said.

"Let's go back *now*," Carter whispered. For reasons beyond me I was ready to agree, but Jack Splint appeared beside us, tall and smiling.

"We're here," he said. "She'll see you now."

We were at the edge of a sort of clearing. At the back of the clearing a hillside dropped down from above, full of trees and brush. I thought I saw, through a tumble of tree trunk, rocks and fern, a hole, like an entrance, or the mouth of a small cave. Something stirred behind the trees, and in the quiet forest evening we could hear the undergrowth rustling.

"Why, look at all the company we're having," Jack Splint said. At that moment a crowd of children parted from the trees, their clothes torn and daubed with glistening dark stains, their faces pale and fixed with a kind of smile, and none of the smiles pleasant at all.

It was the day's class of truant children, a dozen boys and girls I had known for years, fished and hunted or played with and visited on holidays, like stumpy little Joe Scarborough and big-eared Timmy Wales, pretty Suzie Jackman and frumpy Dottie Banks. Now they walked a few steps toward us but stopped, and then resumed, circling us in both directions. A low sound, like growling, rose from them.

"Oh, Lordy," Carter said.

I felt him press towards me for protection. I was the older boy; I had brought him here; I had promised to get him home before dark. In my mind I remembered PawPaw's words the evening before, and my own promise, and being safe in my fortress and PawPaw's arms. Now I saw PawPaw standing on the roof looking down at something as I ran toward school. A gulf in the earth seemed to crack open at my feet, barring me from the trail back to the life I'd known.

"Night's coming on," Jack Splint said.

I looked up. To the east, over No-Name Mountain, wisps of stained clouds, like bloody cloths, wafted across a yellow moon.

"It's late," I said. "I have to see Carter home. I promised."

"Why, a bit late for promises, wouldn't you say," Jack replied, and it wasn't a question. "And here she is."

When I turned around, Emily stood before the dark hole behind the rocks and ferns, still dressed in her white linens, but her clothes were torn and stained and her hair ragged and knotted. She didn't look pretty at all. "Silly boys," she said, her voice deep and liquid, no longer the voice of a child. "Imagine being where you are under a full moon."

"We don't want to be here anymore," I managed to say.

When Emily came toward us, she seemed to glide, her legs and feet motionless beneath her. "Of *course* not," she said. "What silly boy would?"

"Then we'll go now," I said, but my legs wouldn't move. Carter's fingers dug into my arms. Through my cotton shirt I could feel his heart pounding against my back and my own against my chest.

"But you have come for secrets," Emily said. "I, at least, do keep my promises."

She held up two fingers. I shuddered and drew back. Between the webs of her fingers the skin was split and oozing dark blood. Emily's smile widened as the fingers went to her mouth, and her tongue emerged.

"There is only one secret," she said, licking her hand. "Some are *feed*, some are *family*. Only family talks to animals. Feed—well, all must eat or be eaten."

She moved her bloody hand closer to my face.

"One finger or the other—feed or family." As she stared at me the light left her eyes, leaving black wells that had no bottom. "Which are *you*?"

Around us the growling rose to a crescendo. I looked up to see Miss Paltry behind the ring of children and before I could look away I saw the human forms change into terrible misshapen wolf bodies, the hands become claws, the heads grow snouts and fangs and lolling red tongues. When I looked back at Emily she was tall now, old, her leather face cruel above obscene pointed teeth, her hair black as a snake pit. "Or should *Pa* decide?"

Out from the hillside at the back of the clearing, upright strode a horrible yellow-eyed, blood-red wolf, a thousand times larger than the miniature I had seen on the child's bed in the stable. As he approached, the other wildwolves lowered their heads and backed away, still growling and a few beginning to howl. I could not look at the terrible creature as it drew near. Carter had his head buried in my back and his arms clutched around me so tight I could hardly breathe. The red wolf stopped before me and I felt a razor on the tip of my chin, cutting me to the bone, lifting my head upward, so that I was forced to look at him. The wolf put his claw in his mouth and sucked my blood from it, fixing me with his cold yellow eyes.

"I have hunted you longer than I should, little feed," he said, in a voice more like a wolf's than a man's. "All these children were nothing to harvest, yet I thank you for sparing me the work to track this last one down, hiding behind you." Now anger and pleasure mixed in the spittle flowing from his jaws. "But you, thanks to *him*, eluded me too long! That useless crippled feed that built your cabin escaped me too many times in too many years. So did that slippery boy of his, your father! Curse them both! Now let the old feed hobble forever with the leg I *didn't* tear from him during the war that fed us all so well! Let him use the one ear I left him to listen to your mother's wailing! You will serve *me* now, and that will repay his injuries over the years, even this one from last night!"

He took my head in his scaly paw and twisted it upward. I gazed into an oozing tangle of blood clot and hair in the wildwolf's side, where PawPaw must have buried a load of buckshot from his ten-gauge. The creature curled his fangs and snout into a smile. "When he finds you are mine, how will he sleep now, knowing he has lost you?"

"But why," I said, fighting not to burst into tears, "why eat *humans*?"

The red wolf threw his head back and howled a terrible laughter. Beside him Emily hissed, "Not just any humans, if we can help it. Just the *children*."

"But why children?" I insisted. Behind me Carter moaned and buried his head deeper in my back. "Why *us*?"

"Silly boy," the vampire Emily said, leering down at me. "Haven't I already told you? Because the young animals taste so *good*."

Now the wildwolf bent down and put his face against mine. I tried to turn from his foul odor, but those demon eyes sought mine and held me fast. "The old cripple will see that when you promise *me* a thing, you will never neglect to keep it. For *you* will be family, and *this* one"—and he stood and reached behind me and tore Carter free, lifting him screaming and kicking into the air—"will be *feed*."

I reached to save Carter, but before I could grab his legs Emily pulled me upward and sank her teeth into my neck. Over her shoulder I watched as the red wolf twisted Carter's neck sideways and broke it with a loud snap, and then threw the limp form over his back into the middle of the circling, salivating, howling wildwolves.

The last I saw of this natural world Miss Paltry had torn one of Carter's arms from his dead body and held it fast in her snarling jaws, leaving her paws free to fight off Jack Splint and the other wolves reaching to steal her feed away.

***

Thank you for the campfire and the company. Now I should be going, but I do hope you enjoyed my tale. Strange to think I have roamed these woods and others now near a hundred years and never told it before.

And the warning I mentioned at the start of my tale?

Well, we are *everywhere*, and you can never really sleep safely after a night of campfire tales, for who among *your* friends may now be one of us, waiting only for the tiny hours to make *you* feed or family?

Maybe it would be wise to sleep with one eye open.

Oh, and one other thing.

When you promise your grandfather something…

Keep your promise.

Redemption

By Myron Wszelaki

Voted the #2 Best Campfire Story

Marcus and Johnny panted for breath as they ran through the cool desert night. Their hearts pounded wildly and their brows beaded with sweat. Though the bright moonlight illuminated the thinly fogged ground, they still struggled, navigating the scattered rocks and shrubs at such a fast pace. Suddenly, Marcus let out a grunt as he hit the ground, barely catching himself on his hands. Johnny skidded and quickly turned, "Marcus, get up man, get up! They're getting closer!"

Johnny grabbed his shoulder and yanked him up. Marcus's eyes were wide with fear as he huffed out, "What the hell are those things?"

Johnny strained his response, "I don't know… but we're not waiting to find out. Now come on, man!"

He tightened his backpack and again yanked Marcus's arm. The two men resumed their panicked run, racing blindly towards a hope of some safe hiding spot—all the while the savage howls grew louder.

With each painful stride, Marcus's mind reeled with disbelief. How did this happen? How was it that they were now running for their very lives when just minutes ago they were practically home free? He struggled to remember, as if doing so would somehow end this nightmarish reality.

The heist had gone off exactly as planned—no security, no alarms and no problems. He and Johnny grabbed their plunder, jumped into the car and in a few minutes were back on the road. But then Johnny, cocky as always, *had* to show off his driving skills, only he didn't see the veer in the road ahead.

Even though their car didn't "plunge" off the road, it certainly did roll off of it. By the time the brakes screeched, the car was already sliding towards the guardrail. Though their speed was no more than ten mph at impact, the metal rail buckled and their car rolled down the shallow embankment. When it finally stopped, it was with a jolting bump into a very large tree.

But now they were here, terrified and running for their lives—in the middle of a chilled night, in the middle of an empty nowhere, with something vicious closing in fast. Suddenly Marcus gasped and cried out, "Wait! Wa—"

Johnny stopped and again turned. Marcus was hunched over and struggling to breathe. He lifted his head and stammered desperately, "I ca— I can't go on."

Johnny hobbled over and put a hand on Marcus's shoulder. He nudged him urgently, "I know man, I'm fried too. But we gotta keep going. Those things are—"

All of the sudden, the howling stopped. The two lifted their heads and then, with bone-chilling terror, saw *them*. Just a few yards away, atop a low bluff and silhouetted by moonlight, were about two dozen somethings—some sort of creatures. Their frames were the likes of dogs or wolves, but they were bigger—much bigger and horridly more frightening. The large beasts—with eyes ominously aglow—just sat there and glared.

Marcus yelped, "Oh my God! What are those?"

Johnny couldn't answer. He had no answer.

One of the gazing beasts extended its head and then let out a ferocious howl. The rest followed in turn and their shrieks became a deafening din. Marcus's heart pounded in terror and he staggered backwards. Then at once, the horde sprang up and thrust itself down the bluff.

Johnny grabbed Marcus's arm and jerked him into a full sprint. The two were again running, their exhaustion forgotten as adrenaline pumped through their veins with renewed endurance.

The two ran with wild disorientation. Marcus heard the beasts' gargled breathing behind him and any second now, expected jagged jaws to plunge through his flesh and tear him apart. Then something grasped his arm.

Johnny was clenching Marcus's arm and trying to pull him downwards towards a faint glow. He wrenched at Marcus and the two veered into the thickening vegetation below.

Plunging into the thicket, the two flailed their arms and pushed at the tall grasses. And just ahead was the wavering glow. Spent but desperate, the two pumped their legs to their burning limits and finally realized the flicker was a lone campfire centered in a small clearing. Marcus now heard clear footfalls behind him. He snapped his head back and glanced at the thrashing grass trails—the beasts were upon them.

He leapt for the flame.

Johnny was still mid-air when something grabbed his leg; he dropped into the clearing with a thud. He snapped his head back and saw Marcus's writhing face. Marcus's body was only halfway in the clearing and his hands dug into Johnny's leg, pulling at it. But something else was pulling at Marcus. Suddenly, there was a snap and then a yelp, and then Marcus released his grip. He clawed the ground and cried in horror as something dragged him back.

Without a second thought, despite his frozen mind, Johnny sprang around and scurried at Marcus. He grabbed his outstretched hands and steadied himself. He planted his feet in the soft dirt and pulled with all his might. A moment later, Marcus let out a piercing scream and lunged into the clearing—but not alone.

Johnny's eyes went wide at the sight. Latched onto Marcus's foot was a huge, fang-toothed head. Glowing green orbs bulged from a deformed face and drool oozed from its sharp-toothed jaw as it viciously gnawed at its prey. This was no beast; this thing was a monster—a horrid, living nightmare.

Marcus clasped Johnny's hands and cried, "Help me! Help me!"

Johnny pulled as hard as he could, but his hold was slipping as the monster tugged at them. He dared not adjust his grip, for if he did he would surely loose Marcus. But if he didn't, they would both certainly be mauled to death. He had no choice. Johnny's eyes gazed at Marcus with fear and then, he released his grip.

The monster jerked at Marcus with renewed violence as Johnny let go the hand, but Marcus still gripped his other.

Frantically, Johnny clutched Marcus's arm and pulled with the rest of his might. Marcus's body stiffened, then he flew into the opening and crashed into Johnny. The creature's savage grip had broken.

The two madly kicked dirt as they scampered backwards towards the fire. Infuriated, the monster thrust its razored jaws at the two—slashing at the air and snarling madly. Then, realizing its loss, it gleamed at its retreating prey and let out a ghastly howl. Slowly, it drew its horrid head back and vanished into the grasses.

Marcus and Johnny dropped on their backs and gasped for breath. Though right beside it, their panting was heavy enough to drown out even the fire's crackling. Marcus's mind flashed pictures of the green-eyed terror and the snapping jaws of its mangled head. But then, he wondered, why did it not pursue them? Were they still in danger? Would they get out of this alive? He couldn't think straight. He stopped thinking; he just knew that for now they were safe—at least for the moment.

After what seemed like hours, Marcus's breathing slowed. He lifted his head and searched the perimeter. The tall grasses still moved, pushed aside by the prowling beasts. But despite their incessant growling, the monsters did not enter the clearing. Then a sharp thought struck Marcus. He threw off his backpack, jolted upright and grabbed for his foot. "Oh my God! Oh my God! My foot!"

The panicked cry rattled Johnny and he sprang up with a terrified stare. Marcus's eyes were wide as he yelled, but then unexpectedly, he broke a smile of relief—his shaking hands still pointing at his foot. Johnny looked at Marcus's bare foot and shouted, "What? WHAT?"

Marcus gawked at his friend, "LOOK! My foot. Look—it's there—it's still there! I thought it was gone, but it's still there!"

Johnny looked at the shredded pants and his bare foot. He grinned and nodded, "Yeah man, it's still there."

The two sat back down and for a short while neither spoke. But slowly, both again realized their peril and worry wrinkled their faces. The thoughts of the men returned to the lurking pack of monsters out there. Johnny adjusted his backpack, scanned the perimeter and on pure speculation—or perhaps wishful thinking—whispered, "I think they're afraid of the fire. Maybe that's why they haven't come in."

Marcus nodded, distracted, and continued probing his foot, "Hey man, take a look at this, it's odd." He stood up and carefully leaned on his mauled foot.

"What's odd?" asked Johnny.

Marcus looked puzzled. "Well, when that thing had me, I felt its teeth in my skin. I felt it crushing my bones, but look"—Marcus tapped his foot on the ground—"nothing. No pain. No blood. Nothing, not even a scratch."

Johnny smirked in disbelief. "Man, I can't believe you. What did you want, to have your foot be a bloody pulp of shredded meat?" He stood up. "Look man, you got lucky. That thing grabbed you halfway up your calf and shredded your pants. Thank God you were wearing boots. It probably couldn't bite through the leather and just pulled your boot off." Exasperated, he stopped himself and pointed at the perimeter. "Look Marcus, we've got bigger problems. Just be glad you're only missing your boot."

Marcus agreed and dread returned to his face. "So what do we do now?"

Johnny stared at the growling grasses. "I don't know. I guess we just wait till—"

Before he could finish his sentence, a gunshot rang out in the night. Johnny and Marcus hit the ground and the growling stopped. The grasses stirred briskly and then silenced. Johnny carefully lifted his head and listened. After a few moments his face relaxed and he said, "I think they're gone."

Marcus lifted his head and looked around, then anxiously asked, "Well, who the hell fired?"

Marcus scanned the brush and then, beyond the perimeter, he spotted it. In the distance, beyond the grass perimeter, was a shadow. He stared at it and realized it was coming towards the clearing. Marcus ducked and nervously whispered to Johnny, "I think something's coming—coming this way."

Something was.

The shadowy figure was plodding through the grass. Tall and thin, with a large indistinct head, it was heading straight for them. Light played across it as it closed on the fire and it appeared to be human. But its bulky, oversized head was faceless. No nose, no mouth, no eyes. Finally, when it reached the perimeter, its head shifted up—and Johnny and Marcus released their breath.

As the figure crossed into the clearing, its wide-brimmed cowboy hat tilted upwards and revealed a weathered face. Bearded, wearing a long tan overcoat and holding a rifle, it was an old man. Relieved, Marcus and Johnny stood up. Still shaking a bit, Marcus blurted out a "Hello."

The old man, still fifteen feet away, glanced towards them, but ignored the greeting. He rested his rifle against a large rock, pulled a pouch off his shoulder and sat on an old stump. Marcus looked at Johnny, cleared his throat and spoke again, "Ehh, hey mister. Hello."

The old man gave a quick, cold stare towards the fire but again said nothing. He just sat on his stump. Johnny, now annoyed at being ignored, rudely cried out, "Hey mister, what's going on?"

Provoked by his bluntness, the old man sprang up and stepped towards the fire. His searching eyes danced across the two men's pale faces and his eyes gleamed. He looked at Marcus's bare foot. Smirking, he spoke in a raspy voice, "Well I'll be damned. Looks like you boys are in heaping hells of trouble." And with no other word, he turned back to his stump.

The two just stood there, shocked and confused. Johnny frowned and walked over to the old man. "Hey mister, what's your problem? We need some help here."

The old man continued toward his stump. Johnny grabbed the old man's shoulder and barked, "Come on old man, we need some help! Something's trying to get us!"

The old man swung around, flaring with anger. Under different circumstances, he would have already decked Johnny but, restraining himself, he did not. "Like I said, you boys are in a heap of trouble and I sure as hell can't do nothin' about it."

Marcus approached the old man and pleaded, "Come on mister, there're some kind of animals out there trying to get us and we're scared. Please, help us, please."

The old man took his seat and spoke, "I can't help you boys. This here's a very delicate situation. And there's a lot at stake here." He looked at the ground and then back at Marcus. "I'm sorry, boys, I can't help you."

Marcus stood there bewildered. But Johnny, now very frustrated, adjusted his backpack and scanned the quiet, motionless grasses. He touched Marcus's shoulder and spoke, "Come on Marcus, this old codger's crazy. Besides, I think they're gone. Morning's just an hour away so I say we wait till then and go back to—"

A second later, Johnny was on the ground, the taste of blood washed through his mouth. Marcus bent to his friend and looked up. The old man stood there glaring, with his fist in a clench. His coat blew back and he leaned over at Johnny. He spoke sternly, "You are a fool, boy!"

Johnny spit then hollered at him, "What the hell are you doing, mister! We're in trouble here and just wanted some help. Something's after us and we don't even know why. For God sakes, what are you doing? We didn't do anything."

The old man backed up and spoke with contempt, "Oh you did something alright, and you've already paid that price. The question now is what, if anything, you can do to make it right." He turned and muttered, "If you even can."

Johnny got up and wiped his swelling lip. He again grabbed the old man's shoulder and turned to him, only tamer this time. He looked the old man in the eyes as he pleaded. "Listen, mister. I'm sorry. I was out of line. But like Marcus said, we just need some help. We're desperate and scared."

The old man looked at the two for a moment, then begrudgingly, he said, "Listen. I'd like to help you boys but it's…" he paused and stroked his beard, "but it's complicated."

Marcus urged him on, "Please, just tell us, if you know. What are those things?"

The old man paused and took his seat. "Those things, those creatures are called Cheyawa," he said reluctantly. His eyes flashed as he nodded towards the grasses.

"The Cheyawa are a sort of—well, a kind of guardian—but not exactly." He leaned in and continued, "You see, way back when, the Cheyawa were a nomadic Indian tribe. They lived off the lands and pillaged from other tribes. But this wasn't honorable. Legend has it that one day, one of the Cheyawa brutally killed the daughter of an Indian chief. The chief summoned his medicine man to have the murderer cursed, so he could never again harm anyone. The medicine man did as told but instead, he cursed the *entire* tribe. And he cursed them to wander these lands for all time. But not in human form."

The old man paused and threw a grave grin at Johnny and Marcus. "Not as humans, but as horrifyingly disfigured monsters, forever fated to wander these lands and protect the other tribes from the likes of themselves"—the old man leaned in at the men as his eyes flashed with accusation —"from others who were like the Cheyawa. Criminals, like you two!"

A chill ran up Marcus's spine and his heart dropped at the cold words. Did the old man know their secret? Did he know about the stolen goods? The things stashed in their backpacks—how could he?

Johnny quickly looked away and spoke at the ground. "Look old man, that's ridiculous. That's some fool old Indian fable, probably to scare kids or something. Besides, we're not criminals."

But as he lifted his head he met the wide-flared eyes of the old man. "Oh really?" came the scornful response, "then why are they after you, boy?"

Johnny gulped, but before he could get out another denial, a piercing howl broke the silence and the grasses again rustled. Then there was more movement. And then the sinister growls. Marcus jumped up and stared at the brush. "They're back!"

Without a flinch, the old man sneered at Marcus and then finished his story. "Oh yeah, one more thing. Once the Cheyawa find you they will never, never stop stalking you. And when they get you, they *make* you like them—forever!"

Marcus turned white as the blood drained from his head. He stood there in horror, his thoughts jumping to his backpack. Could this be true? Were these monsters really after them because of some stolen Indian trinkets?

Johnny shook as he scanned the perimeter. There were more quick movements within the grasses, then more growling. Then he saw two, then four, then more and more glowing green spots peering at him. And then, a huge werewolf-like head parted the tall grass and pushed itself through. Johnny's eyes widened and his body went limp—the monster was coming in.

Johnny leapt towards the old man, pointed at his rifle and demanded, "Do something you old fool, or you're gonna die with us!"

The old man let out a loud wicked laugh. "Die with you? Boy, you're as good as dead. I'm just here to make sure the *taking* is fair. Nothing else, boy." He laughed even harder as his eyes glowed a faint green.

Panicked now, Johnny swung around and looked at the approaching monster. The lone Cheyawa was in the clearing and heading at them. For the first time Johnny and Marcus saw the hideous creature clearly. It was deformed and grotesque—the size of a man on all fours, but much more bulky. Its writhing muscles bulged as it moved and its long pointed claws punctured the ground with each step. With every flicker of the fire, dark leathery skin gleamed through its short and mangy gray coat, and with each growing snarl, its huge twisted jaw trembled and dribbled with slaver.

The old man riveted his eyes on Johnny and barked over the snarling monster, "You can still redeem yourself, if you want to."

Johnny glared at him with horror and then lunged for his rifle. "You're a fool, old man! And you're gonna die with us!

The old man shook his head and looked at Johnny with regret, then his eyes dimmed and he backed away. Johnny cocked the rifle, pointed and shot at the Cheyawa. Dumbfounded, he looked at the gun, cocked and fired once more. He fired again and again, then finally stumbled backwards and cried in denial—the monster still came.

Just before its pounce, the Cheyawa halted, almost as if wanting to give Johnny one last chance. But terror had gripped Johnny's body and panic had frozen his mind. With shaking hands, Johnny fired a final shot.

In the blink of an eye, the Cheyawa leapt on him and sank its jaw into his thigh. Johnny dropped the rifle and shrieked as the monster thrashed him about the ground. He screamed in agony as his limp hands flopped out at Marcus. "Help me! Marcus, help me!"

The Cheyawa dragged Johnny back towards the grass, then unexpectedly, it paused and gave a green-eyed glare at the old man, almost begging his permission. The old man nodded sadly, then turned his head away. In a blur, the Cheyawa darted into the brush, clutching its screaming prey. Johnny's cries faded in the distance and then, at once, there was silence.

Marcus was horror-struck at what just happened. He just stood there nauseated and quivering. Then, with a horror he never before conceived, he saw his fate approach and wet his pants in fear.

A second Cheyawa had entered the clearing and was heading for him. Marcus, distraught, turned to the old man and cried frantically, "Look! Look out behind you! There's another one. It's gonna kill us!"

Without even a glance back, the old man let out a sigh and tipped off his hat. Then, frustrated at Marcus's ignorance, he spoke to him. "Son. It's like I told your friend. You're already dead. Your only choice now is how you're gonna wind up spending eternity."

He put his hat on and walked towards Marcus, the Cheyawa on his heels. He picked up the dropped rifle and extended it as his eyes flashed a fiery green. "Do *you* want to try your luck?"

Marcus jerked away from the gun and muttered in disbelief, "You're crazy, old man. It's right behind you! It's gonna kill us!" He continued backing away and shouted, "It's gonna kill *me*!"

The old man stopped and gave Marcus a deep glare. Then with bone-penetrating intention, he spoke. "Marcus—*you are already dead.* You and your buddy died less than an hour ago. Remember? When you slammed into that tree, you died. You are already dead. I'm just here to give you a last chance for redemption."

A sharp chill jabbed up Marcus' spine. He stopped and with watering eyes, cried out in disbelief. "What do you mean, dead? I don't believe you!"

The old man tipped his hat again and ran a hand through his white hair. Then he smirked and pointed down, "Look."

Marcus looked down and his world reeled. While edging away from the old man, he had unwittingly backed into, and was now standing in the middle of the blazing campfire—he was on fire. Then he realized something was very wrong—he had no sensation. Nothing. No heat. No burning. No pain. He popped his head up and gawked at the smirking old man.

"Now, son, what are you gonna do?"

In an instant and with shocking clarity, the evening's events flashed through Marcus's mind: Just hours ago, he and Johnny had swiped their goods from the small shop. The antique charms—nothing but ornately-stung beads and a few small animal carvings—would easily be sold to collectors. Easy money, as Johnny put it. They had popped the display case, grabbed the dusty trinkets, and minutes later were back in the car. No one in the sleepy Indian village had seen them.

Soon they skidded off the dirt road and were back on the interstate, home free. Then, just a few miles down the road, Johnny lost control of the car, broke through the railing and careened into the tree. The car was utterly smashed and the windshield shattered, but miraculously, neither one of them was hurt. Not even a scratch.

Marcus's eyes twitched with grim realization. Baffled, he looked up from the cold fire and muttered, "But we weren't hurt."

The old man cracked a smile and nodded him on. "That's right, not *hurt*. And then what?"

Marcus's brow wrinkled as he strained at the memory: they had gotten out of the car, grabbed their backpacks, and were making their way up the embankment. Halfway up they saw it, a large animal at the road's edge. Marcus recalled thinking it was just a large dog or stray coyote. But then, it turned its glowing head at them and shrieked a ghastly howl.

Only startled at that time, the two bounced back towards the car. Johnny's door wouldn't open and he shouted for Marcus to grab the flashlight. Marcus stumbled on something as he reached through the crushed door, grabbed the light and shined it on the ground. He gagged at what he saw—a severed leg, mangled and still wearing its bloodied boot. He dropped the light and stumbled down.

Johnny was already down the hill and shouting urgently, "Come on, man! There's more of them!" Marcus glanced at the road and saw a dozen of the large creatures peering down, wailing with their eyes aglow.

"We ran and ran and then…" Marcus stared blankly at the old man as his memory skipped ahead: the beast mauling his leg; the shredded pants with his bare foot intact; Johnny's final cries as the monster heaved him away; the painless fire.

Then a dreadful grimness overcame him as he whispered, "I'm not dead? Maybe I *am* dead. NO, I'm not."

The old man's jarring laughter interrupted his sluggish realization. He threw his hands up and let out an emphatic "*Duh*! That's what I've been telling you, man. *YOU ARE DEAD*!"

Marcus just stood there, frozen in the shimmering fire. Still laughing, the old man turned his back, brought his arms down and headed for his stump. He passed the drooling Cheyawa and nodded. Instantly, the monster jumped up and resumed its approach. Unable to think and unwilling to move, Marcus knew he was about to die—again. Only this time a more horrible, more agonizing death—like the legend—just like Johnny.

Marcus's jaw hung open in disbelief as he stared into the glassy green orbs of his sure-to-be mutilator, and then back at the old man. Suddenly, in a blinding flash, he realized his salvation. "Wait!" he yelled.

The old man stopped—the Cheyawa didn't.

"Wait, old man. Wait!"

The old man turned and looked at Marcus. His eyes were now glowing intensely, that same eerie green as the beast. Marcus reached a trembling hand over his shoulder, pulled off his backpack and extended his arm.

He fixed his eyes onto the old man's face and stepped out of the fire; then he glanced at the approaching monster and stopped. The old man snapped his fingers and the Cheyawa perched itself. Marcus resumed his nervous walk, passed the beast and reached the old man. He handed the backpack to the old man. At once, something overcame Marcus.

As he gave up the backpack, he was overwhelmed with a strange calmness—a euphoric serenity. The old man smiled and without taking his glowing eyes off Marcus, took the backpack. Marcus tried to return the smile, but only managed a crooked grin back.

Whether it was the sun dawning, or the old man actually emanating a glow, Marcus covered his eyes as a bright, soothing whiteness washed over him. Then, at once, the light faded and Marcus lowered his arm. The old man was gone and in front now stood an old Indian chieftain—traditionally dressed, his body colorfully adorned and his head plumed in feathers.

The Indian peered deeply at Marcus, and then with warm, but spine-tingling words, he said, "You did well, son." He nodded. "You have found your redemption."

As he smiled, he placed his dark arms upon Marcus's shoulders, raised his head to the sky and with foreign words, sang to the heavens. When he finished his chant, he lowered his arm and gazed at Marcus—comfortable green eyes penetrating deeply into his settled soul. With tranquil finality, the old Indian reached a hand towards Marcus's face and whispered as he gently closed Marcus's eyes.

"Ayiwana wadu-heya, Marcus. Ayiwana wadu-heya."
"Rest in peace, Marcus. Rest in peace."

Sleep With One Eye Open

By Kelly Reno

Voted the #3 Best Campfire Story

The sun sank beyond the towering pines of the forest. Chris and Joe had worked all afternoon setting up the perfect campsite by the side of the river. Now it was time to relax for the evening. The propane lanterns were lit and the big green tent had been pitched. Joe was poking a stick at the crackling campfire burning within a circle of river rocks. "Get the hot dogs out of the cooler and bring them out here!" he called to his friend Chris, a first-time camper.

Chris lifted his body up from a pile of sleeping bags that he'd been resting on. "Okay, okay," he groaned, handing the package of hot dogs to Joe. "That was the most work I've ever done in my life! I sure hope you can cook because I'm starving."

Joe stuck the end of a sharpened stick into a hot dog and handed it to Chris. "Just hold it over the fire until it's done," he explained. "Doesn't it give you a feeling of satisfaction—to be up here in the mountains, fending for yourself?"

Chris leaned back on a boulder and stared up at the dark sky. "Yeah. I guess it does. You know what I don't understand, though?"

Joe took a bite of his hot dog. "What?"

"How did those old time prospectors have the energy to look for gold after they set up camp?"

Joe laughed. "Don't worry, you'll have plenty of energy after we find our first nugget of gold in the river tomorrow." He popped open two cans of soda and handed one to Chris. "And now, for a little entertainment."

Chris sat up. "What, you brought the Game Boy?"

Joe rolled his eyes. "Even better. I'm gonna tell you a story. Guaranteed to freak you out."

"Oh yeah? You think you can scare me? I dare you!" Chris challenged.

Joe grabbed a flashlight. "You're on!" he said, positioning the flashlight on the ground so the light shone upwards, casting a creepy shadow on his face.

"Ooooh. Pretty scary, Joey! I want my mommy!" Chris laughed.

Joe began, speaking slowly so that every word would sink in. "There's this campground up here. Fifteen years ago a school group of twenty kids and a couple of grown-ups came up for some weekend hiking. So, they're trekking up this pretty steep trail and one of the kids falls down and twists his ankle. He can't make the rest of the hike. So one of the grown-ups sends him back to the campsite, which is only about two hundred yards from where they are. It's so close that they can even see the tops of their tents. Well, this kid hobbles down the trail and the rest of them go on with their hike. About two hours later, the group returns and they can't find the kid. They tear the place apart looking for him, but he's missing and he stays missing all night. The next day, they still can't find him. He vanished without a trace. There was no sign of a struggle or anything, he just disappeared. Finally, one of the kids finds something off to the side of the trail. It's the camera that belonged to the missing kid. And, on that film was something so horrible, so terrifying…"

Chris was leaning over the fire on the edge of the boulder. "Yeah? He actually took a picture of it? Whoa! What was on the film?"

Joe suddenly jumped to his feet and thrashed around screaming, "A picture of your ugly face!"

Outraged, Chris leapt across the fire pit where Joe was rolling on the ground laughing. "You idiot! You didn't scare me!"

Joe was doubled over, still laughing. Chris punched him on the arm and pinned him to the ground, twisting his fingers backwards. "Say 'uncle', you sorry bag of slime!" Chris shouted.

Joe pushed Chris off him and pointed in his face. "You fell for it! I had you going!"

Chris was about to dive on top of Joe again when his body suddenly froze. His eyes fixed on something in the woods. "Joe! Get up. Get up, Joe."

Joe rose from the ground, brushing the dust off his jeans. "Oohhh. Trying to freak me out? Well it won't work! It—"

And then Joe saw it too. "What the…!"

A dark figure slowly and silently emerged from the thick woods towards the boys. The light of the full moon outlined the ghastly thing as it moved closer and closer.

Chris's voice squeaked, "Who's there?"

Fear itself willed Joe to pick up a heavy rock as a weapon. "Who's out there?" he shouted.

Joe and Chris nearly jumped out of their skins as the figure stepped into the light of the campfire, revealing its leathery face. The ancient mountain man tipped his worn hat to the boys. "Howdy! Name's Lucky."

Chris extended his shaky hand. "You nearly scared us to death, Lucky. I'm Chris, and this is Joe."

Joe winced at the smell of liquor wafting from the old guy. "Yeah. Hi."

Glancing through the opening of the tent, Lucky surveyed the gear within. "Looks like you boys are planning on looking for gold, judging by them pans you got in your tent. Yup. I know most everything about it. Been doing it for over fifty years."

Joe closed the flap on the tent. He didn't like the old man looking at their stuff.

Lucky turned toward the woods and hollered, "Albert! You get down here right now before I have to come and remind you who's boss!"

The boys laughed with relief as a pathetic old burro stumbled down the hill, nearly tipping over under its heavy pack of blankets and tin cooking pans.

Chris whispered in Joe's ear, "The poor guy looks like he should be in a nursing home! Should we give him some food?"

Joe thought about it for a minute and figured that maybe they could coax the old-timer to share a few prospecting tips. "Sure. You ask him."

Chris cleared his throat, "Uh, Lucky? Do you want a hot dog?"

Lucky tied the burro to a tree and smiled toothlessly. "That's mighty kind of you, boys. Don't mind if I do."

Chris went in the tent to get some more hot dogs and chips from the cooler.

Joe watched as Lucky rubbed his grimy hands together over the fire. "So Lucky, do you live up here?" Joe asked.

Lucky cackled like a madman. "No, boy! I live in New York City! I'm just here on vacation. It's been one heck of a vacation, though. Suppose I should write to my mama.."

Chris returned with a hot dog for Lucky. "Here you go."

The burro brayed.

"Keep yer big trap shut, Albert!" Lucky snorted. "I didn't hear nobody inviting you to dinner!" The old man grabbed a handful of potato chips and continued talking. "As I was saying, I came out here fifty years ago looking to strike it rich. A friend of mine heard about a gold mining operation up in these parts, so we made our way out here on freight trains. Got ourselves jobs working as tunnel diggers. Heck, we was as green as you two boys when we got here, but we did what we was told and got the hang of it soon enough. But then things got real bad."

"The gold ran out?" Chris asked.

Lucky took a swig from a battered metal flask. "Oh, no. The gold didn't run out. No sir'ee. It's still up there in that canyon."

Joe coaxed him to go on, "What happened?"

Lucky squinted and shook his head. "Gold does some mighty strange things to men. It can turn nice folks into madmen," he hissed. The old man spat in the fire and narrowed his eyes at the boys. "And it can turn madmen into demons!"

The campfire popped loudly causing Chris to jump.

"You boys ever hear the tale about the Hell's Mouth gold mine?" Lucky asked.

"No," Chris answered. "Would you tell us about it?"

Lucky helped himself to another hot dog, spearing it with a razor sharp hunting knife. "I'll tell you under one condition," he growled.

Joe swallowed hard. "What?"

Lucky narrowed his eyes, "You boys have to promise that you won't go looking for it. It's cursed and it's pure evil. You boys promise to stick to the rivers."

Chris crossed his fingers behind his back. "Okay."

Joe nodded and rolled his eyes. "All right."

Lucky slyly glanced over at his old burro and snapped, "And you cover your flea-bitten ears!" Leaning over the fire, he continued with the story. "Back in the old days, these hills was crawling with mines and miners and even more rumors. Some said that the Hell's Mouth gold mine was the entrance to the mother lode. Others say it was the entrance to Hell. They called it Hell's Mouth because it was the hardest mine to get to and if you worked there, you were vowed to secrecy so that no one would discover its location. There was this greedy crew chief that ran the mine. He worked his men like slaves. They say he found a huge vein of gold and murdered his own crew, one by one, with his pickaxe. Now I don't know if that's exactly how it happened. But I do know this. No one who worked there ever came back alive. They say that old miner's still up there, his eyes as red as the fires of Hell, his clothes nothing but tattered rags and his skin as black as coal. Sealed himself in and hid the entrance. He's still protecting the fortune he believes is rightfully his."

Chris had to hold back a wave of laughter. He leaned back on a sleeping bag. "Have you ever seen him?"

Lucky stood up and brushed his worn leather trousers off. "Don't have to. I know he's up here. I just stopped by to warn you boys. The Hell's Mouth Miner is on the prowl!"

Joe sighed. The tale of an elderly demon prospector wasn't exactly the kind of information he'd hoped to pump out of the old guy. "Thanks for the warning," Joe said flatly.

Lucky untied Albert and led him into the woods. "One last thing, boys!" he called. "Weekend prospectors like yourselves often disappear into thin air up in these parts! He's got his ways of luring young men into his trap if he thinks they're after his gold! *You best be sleeping with one eye open*!"

Chris couldn't stand it any longer and burst into laughter as Lucky hobbled back into the woods. He threw a rock into the river and turned to Joe. "What a lunatic! That guy was so drunk he couldn't even tell a decent campfire story! Your story was scarier than his!"

Joe grinned and gazed up at the starry sky. "But what if it's real? What if there really was a mine like that?"

"Yeah," Chris whispered. "Imagine, all that gold up there just waiting to be found."

Sleep with one eye open…

***

The campfire had died down to a pile of glowing red embers. Inside the tent, Chris and Joe munched on marshmallows. The lanterns cast dancing shadows across the walls of the tent.

"So, do we have everything we need for tomorrow?" Chris asked, poking through the pile of gear.

"I think so," Joe told him, rubbing his weary eyes. "But I still need to read up on how to pan for gold. I think one of the books explains it. Where are the books, anyway?"

Chris rustled around under his pillow and duffel bag. "Right here." He tossed the book to Joe.

Just above the campsite on a rugged mountain trail, a hulking dark figure moved silently toward the tent below. Eyes watched the silhouettes moving through the canvas, sensitive ears listened to every word…

Joe flipped through the pages of the book. "Huh. Let's see if we can find a trail to that old gold mine Lucky was talking about. See if you can find something on that map over there."

Chris ran his finger across the map. "Hell's Mouth Canyon! Look! It's right here. About five miles up the river! It was a real place!"

Joe was reading something in the book with great interest. "It's in this book too, the legend of the Hell's Mouth Miner. I don't believe it!"

"What does it say?" Chris asked.

"It says—" Joe suddenly stopped reading and crawled towards the flap of the tent. "Shhhh. I thought I heard footsteps out there," he said, peering out into the darkness.

"You think it's Lucky again?" Chris whispered.

"I don't know. I don't hear it anymore."

Chris wasn't worried. "It was probably just an animal. Go on with the story. So it really exists?"

Joe pulled a pocketknife out of his backpack. "Just in case," he cautioned, then picked up the book and continued. "It says that many prospectors have searched for the legendary mine near the mouth of the canyon, but no one has ever been able to locate it. The legend says that there's an old cemetery up there where all the murdered miners were buried and that the spirits of the dead men are still searching for the gold. On stormy nights, they say you can see the dead men guarding the canyon when the lightning flashes."

Chris was excited. "Cool! Creepy, but cool."

"We might actually find it," Joe whispered. "Can you imagine?"

Chris flopped down on his sleeping bag. "Man! I wish we could go out there right now and get started. It's torture! Like waiting for Christmas morning."

Joe blew out the lanterns. "I know what you mean. Let's try to get some sleep. We've got a big day ahead of us."

Joe buried his head in a pillow to drown out the sound of Chris's snoring, but it didn't help. Lucky's warning flashed through his mind…

Sleep with one eye open…

Joe finally threw a shoe across the tent. "Be quiet over there! I can't sleep!"

Chris groggily shook his head. "What? Is it morning yet?" he slurred.

"No. It's the middle of the night. You're making too much noise," Joe snapped.

"Whatever," Chris mumbled.

Joe sighed heavily, then suddenly sat up, straining to listen to the noise outside the tent of crunching gravel. He opened the tent and searched through the darkness with his tired eyes. Black clouds had moved in and the sky rumbled with a boom of thunder.

Joe shook Chris by the shoulders. "Put your shoes on. There's something weird going on out there!" he hissed.

Joe turned on the flashlight. "Come on, Chris!"

***

Moments later, Joe and Chris were creeping toward the river, through a mist of fog that was rolling in through the canyon.

Chris tugged on Joe's jacket. "What if it's the spirits of the dead miners? What if they're warning us to stay away?"

Drops of rain began to fall.

An icy chill ran down Joe's spine. *No, it couldn't be*, he thought. But what in the hell had been walking around out there? He was sure he'd heard footsteps.

Chris glanced up the riverbank.

"Look! Over there!" Joe whispered, pointing to a gravel pit on the other side of the river where several dark shapes stood.

Squinting through the fog, Chris feared that his heart might explode with fear. There was definitely something out there. Something big—and there was more than one of them.

Joe grabbed Chris and pulled him behind a large boulder, where they peered out at the black figures across the river.

"What are they?" Chris panicked, his every muscle frozen with terror.

Suddenly, a blinding white light flashed across the sky.

Chris and Joe screamed, "Aaaaaaaugh!"

The dead miners!

Joe looked up, nearly blind with fear. Then he saw the four deer at the edge of the river dart off into the forest.

"It was just some deer!" Joe howled with laughter. "Just some stupid deer!"

Heart still thudding, Chris took a deep breath and started laughing too. "Come on. Let's get out of here."

As they headed back toward the campsite along the riverbank, Joe spotted something sparkling in the water. He grabbed a stick and poked at the glistening object that was wedged between two rocks. Reaching out, Joe wrapped his fingers around it. "A bottle," he sighed. "Just an old bottle."

He held the amber glass beneath his flashlight and noticed that this was no ordinary bottle. It was very old, maybe even an antique. "Chris, look what I found in the river."

Chris looked the bottle over. "Is it worth anything?"

"Maybe," Joe said. "I'll take it to one of the antique shops next week and see."

***

Back in the tent, Chris inspected the bottle by the light of the lantern. "There's something inside of it. Looks like paper."

"Oh yeah?" Joe said. "Open it up."

Chris carefully removed the cork. "Give me something to get this out with."

Joe tossed his pocketknife to Chris. "Be careful," he warned. "Don't mess it up or anything."

Chris gently pulled the edge of the yellowed paper out and Joe watched as he carefully unrolled it.

The blood drained from Chris's face.

"What is it, man?" Joe questioned. "What does it say? Chris?"

With a limp hand, Chris passed the paper to Joe.

His eyes traveled across the faded letters. "Oh my God," he breathed. "This can't be real."

"It can't be," Chris whispered, his eyes fixed on the rising flames.

Joe read the paper one more time and took a deep breath. "It's a map to the entrance of the mine! Hell's Mouth Gold Mine!"

"I bet Lucky planted it there to freak us out," Chris argued.

"But look at the paper, and the writing, and the bottle we found it in!" Joe pointed out. "This is authentic! You couldn't fake a document like this! Do you realize what this means?"

"I have the feeling I'm about to find out," Chris answered uneasily.

Joe stood up and held the map up victoriously and screamed like a madman. "Awooooooo! This means that we're holding the key to the big one! The mother lode!"

The spark of madness in Joe's eyes scared Chris a little bit. He remembered what Lucky had said... *It turns nice folks into madmen... And madmen into...* Chris shuddered, shaking the thought from his head. "Be quiet!" he hissed. "Somebody might hear you. We'll go check it out tomorrow. All right?"

BOOOOOOOOM!

Thunder cracked across the sky, followed by a flash of lightning that illuminated the inside of the tent for a moment, making the crazed expression in Joe's eyes visible.

Then a dark figure flashed across the dirt just beyond the open flap of the tent. Joe and Chris both poked their heads outside, searching though the mist surrounding the dark forest around the campsite.

"Did you see that?" Joe hissed, scrambling to his feet. "There's somebody out there!"

"It's probably just those deer again," Chris whispered.

Joe quickly stuffed the map back in the bottle and tucked it inside his sleeping bag. "Who's out there?" he shouted, emerging into the fog outside. "I said WHO'S OUT THERE?" he screamed.

"Get back in the tent!" Chris pleaded. "You're acting crazy!"

"Crazy!" Joe laughed manically. "CRAZY!"

Unsure of what to do, Chris burst out of the tent and stood on shaking legs next to Joe. "You need to chill out, Joe!"

Before Chris could figure out what to do next, a dark figure emerged from the trees and growled—the dry, rotting sound of something inhuman.

Chilled to his very bones, Chris's eyes darted around for something to use as a weapon. Joe had been right. There was something out there.

The thing was just yards away from the tent, but it was too dark and foggy to make out what it was.

"What is it?" Chris whimpered.

The thing moved closer, the stench and heat of its breath wafting through the fog.

The two boys seemed to wilt before the evil presence among them. "It's not a deer!" Joe panicked.

"Who's out there?" Chris hollered, eyes madly scanning the dense trees.

But there was no reply, only another deep, guttural growl, followed by heavy footsteps of the black mass that was moving closer and closer.

"M—might be a bear," Joe stammered.

"Or maybe Lucky's back," Chris gulped.

But they were both wrong. As another bolt of lightning flashed across the sky, their question was answered when they saw the gleaming point of a pickaxe clutched in the hands of a monster with eyes as red as the fires of Hell.

***

Joe and Chris were never seen again. The officials reported the incident as a missing person's case, but those familiar with the legend of the Hell's Mouth Miner knew otherwise.

Beware the lure of gold for it turns nice folks into madmen and madmen into demons!

Night Gobblers

By Bob Sullivan

Can you tell when someone is watching you, even before you see them? Some people can, at least some of the time.

Can you tell when something is watching you in the night and wants to kill and eat you, even before you see it, hear it or smell it? Most people can, though they may not acknowledge it.

There you are, taking out the trash at night, in the dark, just like you have many times before. Suddenly you feel something dangerous and just about terrifying. The fear starts on the back of your neck, shoots to your stomach and then creeps down your legs. It's an ancient fear that can't be stopped or dealt with except by moving away from its source—fast! (Well, there are other ways to stop it if you're confident enough—but more on that later.) You hastily throw the trash in the can and rush back into the house. You tingle with the thrill of your escape and the relief of a safe, warm shelter where the eyes can't see you. You make sure the door is well locked so it can't get in. You never bother to mention any of this to anyone.

What was watching you? What was projecting that fear? The not-knowing is bad enough. But the worst part is the feeling that if the thing ever jumped out and grabbed you, you would be overwhelmed with terror and become utterly paralyzed, totally helpless, and be torn to bits by it.

One of man's age-old nightmares is of being chased by an overwhelmingly dangerous *something*, and not being able to run. But *this* is not a dream—you're wide awake.

Almost all of us have felt this fear, out of doors, in the night. If you haven't, then go out in the woods by yourself, miles from safety. Walk around in the dark for a while. Take all of the clubs or knives you want, the fear will still find you. The thing will still be watching you.

The fear is so real, so ordinary, that some people get the creeps just thinking about walking alone at night in the woods. Would you like to take a long, lonely stroll in the dark wilderness right now? Go ahead; we'll wait by the campfire for you.

There is one bit of good news to keep in mind: even though we often sense It, *It*, the fear maker, very rarely shows itself or actually attacks. But when it does… well, here's a tale about one such attack.

***

Jeff Adler knew wild turkey hunting inside out and he knew turkeys were the hardest animal to hunt in North America. They have hearing and eyesight a dozen times sharper than ours and they are constantly on the lookout. Their only weakness is a pretty girl—or rather, a pretty hen turkey.

During the spring mating season the boys ("toms") will drop their guard. If you can do a good job of pretending to be a hen, you can get a tom to walk within easy shooting distance, thirty yards or less.

All six-foot-four inches of Jeff Adler didn't look much like a hen turkey. To fool a tom, Jeff had to sound like a hen and look like a bush; in other words, he had to totally blend in with the woods, be perfectly still and completely quiet. A wild turkey can see a man's eye blink at one hundred yards and hear a soft sneeze at two hundred yards—even in thick forest.

The night before the opening day of Missouri's spring turkey season, Jeff gathered all his camouflage paraphernalia and got ready for the hunt. Every inch of his body, clothes and gun were covered in some sort of clever camouflage. He put special camo tape on the shot-gun's barrel and stock, camo paint on his face and a camo net covered his eyes (to hide the blinks, of course).

He had a small cushion to sit on, clothes, a shotgun, a turkey caller and that was it. There was no need for food, water or toilet paper because eating, drinking and "going" were not possible until after the hunt.

Jeff's turkey caller fit entirely inside his mouth. To imitate a lonely hen looking for a fella, Jeff only had to open a small crack between his lips and blow softly over the caller. The sound had to be an exactly perfect duplicate of a hen turkey or no tom would come.

Jeff had spent years perfecting his call. He was able to sit for hours without moving. If you call well, any tom in the area is likely to be looking right at you. Just a few clucks on the caller can get them looking. If you move at all—even slightly—they will see you and stay away. If you are perfectly still and you are well camouflaged, they *can't* see you and they will come closer to find the "hen."

Jeff loved everything about the sport except for one thing: you usually can't set up on a calling location during the daylight. Every turkey within a mile will hear you coming into the woods and then you're defeated before you start. Turkeys sleep in trees at night and spend most of the day pecking around on the forest floor. To set up for a turkey hunt you'd better be in the woods well before sunrise. Jeff did not like being in the woods alone at night. Not many people do.

Jeff's family farm was 480 acres of pasture and crop fields but mostly it was dense, hilly Ozarks oak forest. Jeff knew every inch of it and enjoyed every inch except for "The Gulch," his name for the forty acres out behind the pond. There was something spooky and unwelcoming about that place even in the daylight. He never liked going there. But this year he knew that most of the turkeys on his property were roosting there every night and it was his best chance, perhaps his only chance, at bagging a big tom.

Jeff left the house at 3:00 a.m. He was nervous but resolute as he gave his sleeping wife a goodbye kiss on the head. Had he known what awaited him in the woods, he would have stayed by her side.

***

Jeff had scouted the gulch in advance and figured he knew which tree the turkeys were now using as a night roost. One hundred yards away he had picked out an excellent spot to hunt from: three trees close together with low hanging branches and lots of underbrush. Just before first light he planned to call a few times to the birds up in their tree roost. This would get a tom or two headed his way when the flock flew off the roost. Sometimes a flock will come off the roost just before first light, while it is still pitch black. Of course you can't shoot until you have enough light to see by, but you can still get the toms walking your way even in the blackness.

Turkey hunts are often slow, long, patient things. Toms can pinpoint a hen's call at 5:00 a.m., make their first move in "her" direction at 5:30 a.m. and take three hours to meander the one hundred yards to where they think she's at.

Or, a tom can come directly off its roost, fly straight for the concealed hunter and land on the hunter's head before the hunter has a chance to make even a second call. In this situation twenty pounds of bird and 180 pounds of hunter proceed to scare the holy hell out of each other. Bird and man literally can't get away from each other fast enough and pound one another vigorously in the attempt. Then, after they have flailed in one screaming, gyrating spot for untold seconds, their first lunges to escape will find them both (as a unit or separately) smashing headlong into the nearest tree, or perhaps several trees in succession. By the time the hunter figures out what's happening, all chance at a shot is gone and so is the turkey. Wives find these encounters endlessly humorous and so very few stories of this type ever leave the woods.

Needless to say, Jeff would always prefer a three-hour contest of stealth to having a bird land on his head. But this night was to be a contest of another sort.

***

The fear found Jeff soon after he parked the pickup and entered the gulch. A twelve-gauge double barrel loaded with magnum shells is an awesome confidence builder, so Jeff was able to hold off the fear for a while—a little while.

Jeff had noticed many "undocumented phenomena" during his decades of hunting. Some of them were the secret weapons used by owls, foxes and other killers in the woods. Rabbits, quail and the like can disappear in the underbrush simply by remaining perfectly still. The best vision in the animal kingdom can't find perfectly camouflaged prey as long as it doesn't move. Smell only works if the wind direction is just right. Secret Weapon #1 is to bombard a likely area with a beam of panic so that prey cannot resist moving—making a break for it. Then, once the prey has flushed into the open, Secret Weapon #2 is to move closer to the prey and bombard it with a beam of terror so intense that the prey freezes.

Jeff had seen these things and wondered why science never mentions such. Hawk flies over, rabbit bursts from a perfect hiding spot, hawk swoops down, rabbit-paralyzes and is easily picked up—fast food, hawk style.

Another secret weapon seemed to be a pervasion of an area by a predator which wards off intruders; a "stay-away-or-die" vibe set up in the territory of a killer to warn off competing killers. Jeff knew that some predators stake their territories with pee but there was more to it than pee. Jeff could sense the repelling vibes of some predators. Why had biologists never recorded these things? Jeff reckoned scientists must not know much about life. Anyway, the vibe Jeff felt tonight was extreme—way beyond anything usual in those woods. It made him aware of an impending fight to the death with something monstrous. "Get out or die" was pushing its way through any shotgun bravado. This was no fox or raccoon territory. This was horrible and Jeff felt like going back home. Now! But hunters didn't do that.

Two years prior a turkey hunter had been found slashed to ribbons in the next county. His dead face was frozen in an expression of unspeakable horror—at least what was left of it. The undertaker couldn't do much for it. Jeff's brother saw the body before the casket was closed and said something from Hell was loose in the Ozarks.

Jeff didn't believe in Hell during daylight hours, but the thing pushing on his awareness now was definitely not from Heaven. Jeff knew if he backed out of the gulch now he could never be master of his land again. He determined to use his sharp awareness of this monster, whatever it was, to beat it. And then there was the original business of bagging a turkey.

Jeff crept through the blackness toward his hunting spot. He occasionally flicked on a pen-light to get his bearings amongst familiar landmarks but was aware that his light would only give away his location to whatever might be out there.

He found his spot with no real trouble, put down his cushion and settled in for the contest. At 5:15 he made his first cluck. Then *all* eyes were on him. He heard the flock fly to the ground and one tom began gobbling. A gobble says, "Here I come, baby, you can't resist my manly charms, and all other toms get out of my way or I'll kick your ass."

Jeff could hear the tom very slowly wandering in his direction. In ten minutes he'd have enough light to barely see by—but then it happened!

The continuous get-out-of-here fear Jeff had been feeling turned into panic. The wavelength of the vibe changed and suddenly Jeff knew he was being hunted as prey. He broke out in sweat, wanted to scream, wanted to run; he absolutely *had* to run—but he didn't—he was there to hunt, not be hunted.

The killer had sensed Jeff's entrance into the woods but pretty much ignored it. Humans taste bad—or at least they smell like a very bad meal. The killer lost Jeff's scent as Jeff moved downwind. Now it was time to gobble a few gobblers or hens.

The killer heard the flock fly down and heard a lonely hen in the distance. An easy plan: quietly grab the hen, then move in on one of those silly sex-crazed toms. He pinpointed the hen's position by sound but couldn't see it, even with incredible night vision. He needed to get that hen to move, even a little, to zero in on the exact kill spot.

The killer turned up its panic beam. Nothing happened.

Jeff felt the beam hitting him harder and harder. He *had* to flee! But the tom was within fifty yards and still coming slowly. He'd have shooting light in about five minutes.

The monster turned up the power even further and still nothing. This was no hen. Whatever it was had defied him and he was now going to revel in ripping it apart.

Jeff was locked into more intensity than he could deal with. He had to run—had to. But as the hunter, he had to stay exactly still.

One more cluck of the caller. The monster moved closer, slamming the spot with panic, but couldn't see its prey. Jeff almost screamed. He couldn't see, hear or smell the killer but knew it was coming. *Got to run.*

The tom moved out from behind a tree thirty yards away just exactly as the first grey of morning gave enough light to aim by.

Jeff pulled his shotgun to his shoulder and pulled the trigger in one motion. Three or four of the #4 shot found the bird's head and penetrated. The turkey flopped over.

Exactly then the monster saw its prey move—finally. The monster turned on Weapon #2 and paralyzed Jeff with terror.

Jeff saw his tom flop down dead, then he was smashed with overwhelming fear. Images of being torn apart throat first and guts ripped out washed over him. Jeff felt like he was already dead and gave up.

The monster lunged for the kill just before he recognized his target as a human.

An instant before impact, Jeff said—*Jeff* said, not some primal instinct or unconscious genetic response—*Jeff* said: "*I'm* the hunter in theses woods," and spun around discharging the remaining barrel of his twelve gauge at the thing flying towards him.

The blast ripped the chest out of the mountain lion in mid-air. Its momentum carried it forward to land at Jeff's feet. Jeff felt a warm liquid running down his leg.

After an unknown amount of time, Jeff surveyed the situation and made his decision. He calmly walked to his turkey, picked it up, walked to his truck and drove home. He knew he was the prime mover on this land and that was the end of it. You see, no mountain lions had been documented by science in Missouri for over one hundred years. The eco crowd would move in and he'd have to "prove" he had killed the lion in self-defense. Since scientists have no real idea what's going on, they'd be out there taking samples or some such silliness and turn his farm into a study-zone or something.

And then his wife—oh my God—surely she would ban all outdoors fun for Jeff and the boys for eternity.

There are some things better left to the woods.

***

Every year a turkey hunter somewhere is mistakenly attacked by a bobcat or some other type of wild animal. Every night thousands of sensitive hunters or hikers get bombarded by an irresistible urge to flee—even some innocent trash taker-outers. Usually it's an owl or a weasel or some predator like that—they just want you to move on, out of their hunting area—or they're just having a little fun with you, or they can't help themselves because that's what they do. Sometimes, for you late-night trash men, it can even be your neighbor's cat—a vicious hunter of the first order.

Solution: turn around and give it right back to them—or, just laugh and say hello. You're the hunter in these woods.

The Dare

By Frank Clark

Jim pulled up his jacket collar; he hated having a cold neck. It was a dark and lifeless night. Dense fog met every contour of the landscape and what scant moonlight there was, illuminated very little. His best friend Danny Miller sat next to him. The boys were spending the night at the Goshen Cemetery, located on a gravel road a few miles outside of town. Jim had told his parents that he was spending the night at Danny's house; Danny had told his parents that he was spending the night at Jim's house.

It wasn't that Jim and Danny were keen on camping in a graveyard. But they did live in a small Missouri town, a place where adventurous eighth-grade boys sometimes needed to come up with something new, to keep from ending up bored like everyone else. And since they had been "dared" to spend Halloween night in the cemetery, they felt a certain compulsion to put the issuer of the dare, a high school freshman, in his place.

They had heard the strange stories about the Goshen Cemetery, a place where some folks felt pretty uncomfortable even during daylight hours. Unexplained, strange occurrences were not rare. Danny reminded Jim about the disappearance, only a year ago, of local jack-of-all-trades (including gravedigger) Layton Barker. Just outside the cemetery gate early one morning, a farmer had found Layton's old Ford pickup truck. The truck's engine was running and the driver's side door was open. But there had been no sign of Layton Barker. The local sheriff had been called out to investigate. He had

found nothing unusual except for a pile of ashes between the truck and the gate. Layton Barker was never found.

Jim and Danny were the best of pals and had been so since the first grade. They always stuck together, no matter what. Enjoying the campfire they had built behind a large tombstone, the two reminisced about some of the good times they had shared. They were laughing, having a pretty good time and were not so much concerned about the fact that they were sitting in an old graveyard out in the middle of nowhere on Halloween night.

Then Danny brought up the fifth grade, the one year both of them had lived in pure Hell at the mercy of a very nasty and unhinged teacher, Mrs. Shipman. A certifiable lunatic, she had not wanted any fifth-grader to have any fun or enjoy life. She had always made it her concern to constantly ridicule and suppress students in her class. She had singled out the most independent students and then had done her best to covertly crush their spirit. Both boys had suffered, Jim especially. Even though they had never seen her flying monkeys, Jim and Danny had no doubt that Mrs. Shipman was the Wicked Witch of the Mid-West. She passed away during their seventh-grade year and was buried at the Goshen Cemetery.

Several hours of conversation and laughter had passed. Jim and Danny could just barely stay awake. Camping in the Goshen Cemetery wasn't a big deal; they could just crawl into their toasty sleeping bags, close their eyes and do some serious snoozing.

They talked for a bit more. Jim turned the topic of the conversation back to Mrs. Shipman. He told Danny that since she was now buried just ten or fifteen feet from where they were sitting, one or two loud farts might just be enough to get her to roll over. They both laughed.

Seconds after the boys had put out the fire and unrolled their sleeping bags, there was a strange occurrence at the Goshen Cemetery. The faint image of an older woman appeared near a gravestone not far away. Both boys saw it and stared. Even though Jim had already pulled up his jacket collar, his neck was still cold and it was getting colder. It was a different kind of cold, one which he'd never before experienced.

Strange! Even though the image was difficult to see in such dim light, Jim and Danny both agreed that it sort of looked like Mrs. Shipman! They were silent but continued to stare at the image, and they were beginning to feel considerably less inclined to go to sleep. They were doing their best to remain calm and that was not easy. And just as quickly as the image had appeared, it then vanished. Jim turned to check out Danny's reaction. Danny was gone!

Jim looked around for Danny; there was no sign of him. Then, without warning, Jim received a sharp rap to back of his right shoulder. He turned to his right, expecting to see Danny. But there was no Danny. Jim didn't see anyone or anything. What the hell was going on? Jim's heart was beating hard and fast.

The image appeared once again, only this time it was not pale. It was Mrs. Shipman; there was no doubt. Jim recognized that covert and forged smile; and there were those piercing, goblin-like eyes. Then he remembered how she would sneak up behind a student who was having a good time in class and rap them on the back of the shoulder with a wooden ruler.

Mrs. Shipman began to move very slowly in Jim's direction. Dealing with the "deceased" Mrs. Shipman was not something that Jim was at all interested in. He wanted to run like hell but he had to find his friend. The pressure got so intense that Jim attempted to temporarily retreat to regain his composure. But that didn't happen. With a rapid surge of speed, Mrs. Shipman was directly in front of him, her amber eyes informing him that he was not yet excused!

The back of Jim's neck felt like ice that never melts. What had happened to Danny? He knew that his best friend would never just bail on him. How could Danny have just vanished? Jim was terrified; he didn't know what to expect. Was he going to die?

Jim looked at Mrs. Shipman. He saw weird "pictures" that were just sort of suspended around her. He saw a picture of Layton Barker closing the cemetery gate. And then he saw a picture of Layton walking to his truck. The one after that was more than Jim could take! It was a picture of Layton Barker's body combusting; there was a blue-orange flame that lasted only a second or two. There were no more pictures, but there was fear with the volume turned up to high. Jim suddenly remembered that Layton Barker had once attended a school board meeting to lodge a complaint against Mrs. Shipman; Layton's son had been a fifth-grader in her class.

Mrs. Shipman was smiling and it was not a becoming smile. And Jim's neck of ice was not thawing. He wondered if this was to be his last night on Earth as Jim Edwards. Would he go out experiencing unbearable pain? Would he end up in some half-world? And who or what else might be there as well, always lurking in the shadows?

Suddenly, the campfire that Jim and Danny had extinguished hours ago instantly came back to life, three times the size it had been. Jim looked at the fire and nearly came unglued at what he saw—Danny's face in the flames! Danny's expression was one of pure terror.

Jim had never before felt so helpless and alone. He didn't know what to do. What the hell was going on? This was certainly the most intense evil he had ever experienced. Jim felt like he was being sucked into a ghastly world with no exit.

Mrs. Shipman very much enjoyed watching Jim come apart. She was quite aware of the effects she was creating. The more Jim surrendered to her, the more power she seemed to have over him. Jim's legs felt like stone; he could move his body only a little. Smirking, Mrs. Shipman faded away.

Something was grabbing at Jim's left foot. He tried to move his foot but couldn't. Then something else was grabbing at his right foot. And there was Mrs. Shipman, floating a foot or so above the ground, circling around behind him. She was laughing and it sounded like something straight from Hell. Jim knew that he would soon be attacked. He felt that he would not see it coming.

He then heard a low-frequency rumbling sound coming from behind. The ground beneath his feet started to vibrate. Then his hands were vibrating; he looked at them in the light of the campfire. His fingers had fused together. Jim's left foot began to kick wildly right before his legs gave out. But his body remained in an upright position. Jim then saw things from a very different point of view. He realized that he was watching his body from above; it was just sort of standing there, supported by some exterior source. He knew that he wasn't that thing he was looking at from above. It was just a body—but it was his body and he wasn't ready to give it up.

A weak voice was calling to him and it was coming from the campfire. It was Danny calling him, telling him to run, to get away from there. Jim tried to move his body; he felt like an amateur trying to work a marionette. His body was not responding. If he just gave up would he then become an unwilling inhabitant, sentenced to a nightmarish eternity in the underworld of his wicked fifth-grade teacher?

Mrs. Shipman looked at Jim's body and then she smiled. What was really hiding behind that smile Jim didn't care to discover. She then looked up and right at him. He couldn't hide and he knew it. She knew it, too. Would he ever again be able to go home and be with his family? Would he ever see Danny again?

In a very brief but intense flash of blue-orange flame, Jim's body was reduced to ashes. But he was still there and he could still see what was going on around him. Mrs. Shipman then spoke for the first time. She said, "Your unwelcome visit here was an unfortunate mistake. So, you might as well learn to adjust; I'm afraid that I shall not ever permit you to leave."

Jim's alarm went off. He opened his eyes, but he didn't get out of bed right away. Looking around his room, he recognized familiar objects. He looked around some more. He looked at his hands. He rubbed them together and then hopped out of bed. The cold floor actually felt good on his warm feet. Both were very real to him and he liked that.

He walked over to look out his bedroom window and saw his best pal Danny coming up the street. That's right; it was Saturday morning and they were going out to shoot some hoops. Jim turned and raced off to put on his clothes. But in doing so he stubbed a big toe on the metal bed frame. It hurt like hell, but Jim was rolling on the floor, holding his injured big toe and laughing his head off!

As he was going down the stairs the doorbell rang. He was more than ready to pulverize Danny in a game of one-on-one. Jim opened the door and was greeted by a smiling and familiar face. But it was not a becoming smile. The visitor looked at Jim for a few moments and then spoke. She said, "How very amusing—did you really think that it was only a dream?"

Old Medicine Woman

By Elizabeth C. Sullivan

Oh-tay-yah was tired. She had been the healer and wise woman for her tribe for thirty summers, longer than anyone else could remember. She was so old now that she could barely see. She realized that some of her recent cures didn't work because she had not enough use of her senses to diagnose what was wrong and what was needed.

She knew all this, but she still loved life. She didn't want to be old. It was not her fault that she was old. Nevertheless, when the tribe moved off to summer camp, she could not keep up. Last year they had carried her. This year, they left her behind to die. She knew it was the tradition, and she expected it to happen. That didn't make the situation any more appealing.

She was supposed to sit on the prairie and sing and wait until death came. What a useless end! Oh-tay-yah felt bitter for a while. She sang her anger at the members of the tribe. She sang her anger at the gods who allowed this to happen after she had been faithful these many years. She sang her anger at her children and grandchildren, and all those she had healed.

Then she cried until she could not cry anymore.

She slept. When she woke up, she thought she might have died, but no, there was her body under her blanket on the plains, in the cold, crisp air.

But she was no longer angry or bitter or sad. After a while she realized she was looking down at her body. The body was sleeping. Was it? It wasn't breathing! So how come she was still there?

She decided to be higher, and she was. Her body was very far below. She decided to peek over the edge of the land. So she moved west and she could see farther. She saw the trail where the tribe had gone.

This is wonderful, thought Oh-tay-yah. I could be anywhere! She drifted a bit, then saw a hawk riding thermals. She followed the hawk and rode with the hawk all day and hunted with it at night.

When riding the hawk, she saw a mountain goat climbing in a place that she always wanted to go, but could never reach. She left the hawk and followed the mountain goat.

While she was with the mountain goat, she saw a chipmunk and wondered where he was going. She followed him into his burrow, but that wasn't very interesting, so she came out.

She drifted upwards and spied a lake where the tribe fished in summer. She shot below the waters of the lake and followed fish until she found herself in a river, with a fish that was about to be dinner for a beaver. She stayed with the beavers for a while.

When she understood the beavers to her own satisfaction, she followed the antelopes, then buffalo, then a bear. Time was nothing. She didn't notice it passing. She understood more than she ever had in her old body. She wanted to tell her family and her tribe. So she started to search for them. Then she realized she didn't have to search, she just had to be there, in the place where the tribe lived. And she was.

She saw her daughter, who was now the Old Medicine Woman of the tribe. The daughter was off by herself, crying. Oh-tay-yah felt compassion. She went to her daughter. Oh-tay-yah knew the woman was crying because one of her patients had died, and now the woman was afraid she would be shunned by the tribe for not being able to cure the little boy who had been sick.

"Don't be afraid. You have nothing to worry about. I will make you the strongest Medicine Woman who ever lived," said Oh-tay-yah.

The daughter stopped crying. She looked around as if searching for someone. Oh-tay-yah knew that her daughter could not see her. Oh-tay-yah tried hard to be visible to her daughter, but she had no body. The daughter could not see the being who was Oh-tay-yah.

"I am Oh-tay-yah, your mother. You will have to trust the voice in your head. My body has died, but I will tell you this secret, daughter. When the body dies, you are free. You can go anywhere. You can be the wind, the hawk, the bear, the fish. So do not mourn for the little boy. Never mourn again for those who pass from their bodies. They are free."

The daughter calmed. She went back to the tribe and called a meeting of the elders and she told them of the revelation she had, away in the prairie. They did not ridicule her because they were old, too, and they wanted to believe. They wanted hope for their own futures. The daughter promised them she would be the best Medicine Woman ever, because not only would the tribe have her help, but they would also have the help of Oh-tay-yah. But never again were they to mourn the dead. They should, instead, celebrate the freedom of a being released.

As days, weeks, years went by, the daughter did become the most remarkable Medicine Woman ever. And because of her skills, with the help of Oh-tay-yah, the members of the tribe began to believe her, that death was a release of the being, and that freedom from the body should be celebrated. Some of the younger ones even claimed to have seen Oh-tay-yah, walking around like a ghost at night. Oh-tay-yah thought that was very funny, since it was obviously something made up to startle their elders.

The daughter taught her own daughter to be the Medicine Woman. Eventually the granddaughter of Oh-tay-yah would take over the duties. While still studying, she became pregnant—she knew it would be a girl.

Oh-tay-yah got the idea to become this new baby. It wasn't born yet, so Oh-tay-yah asked her daughter to ask the granddaughter if she could have the body of the new baby when it was born. Both daughter and granddaughter were thrilled. And when the baby was born, they named her Oh-tay-yah, after the old woman who had died alone on the prairie.

The Back Road

By Lucy Quigley

I know it would be a real cop-out if I told you one of those stories that ends, "And then I woke up and realized it was all a dream," so I'm not going to tell you one of those. I'll tell you something that really happened to me. I don't like to talk about it, and there are those who wouldn't want you to know the truth because they don't want to scare you away from the mountains where it happened. But I think you're braver than that.

***

The summer that I graduated from high school, my best friends and I decided take a camping trip to top all camping trips. It was going to be our good-bye celebration. In a few days, Beth and Vance would both be leaving for college, Mike was moving out of state, and I was taking a job in the city. Even the threat of rain that weekend didn't dampen our enthusiasm for this last hurrah.

It was a Friday afternoon in late August when we loaded up Mike's little Honda hatchback and started on the three-hour drive to the campsite. Or rather, it was supposed to be a three-hour drive, but we ended up getting stuck in a major road-block on the highway and sitting in traffic for hours while we waited to see what was happening up ahead. It was getting dark and a light rain had started.

"What's the deal with all this traffic?" Vance asked for about the sixth time that hour. "Can't you get anything on the radio?"

In the front passenger seat next to Mike, Beth fiddled with the radio knob. "It's been mostly static since the road curved back there."

A loud buzzing noise filled the car as the stations cut in and out. And then suddenly we heard: "Roadblock on Interstate… unauthorized breach… military base… residents warned to be on the lookout for…"

"Military base?" I turned to look at Vance, whose Dad was in the army. "I didn't know there were any military bases around here."

"There aren't," Vance said, frowning. "I mean, except for…" he paused.

"What?"

"Well, there's a top-secret facility of some kind. I overheard my dad talking to someone about it once, when he thought I was asleep. But it's not like a normal military base. I don't think I'm supposed to talk about it."

"We could be in danger here!" Beth's voice rose. "What kind of place was it? What should we look out for?"

Vance shrugged. "I don't really know. All I know is, there was something there that my dad said people would never believe, if they saw it."

We inched up to the roadblock, and Mike rolled down his window as an officer approached the car. He shined a flashlight around at all our faces. "You folks haven't seen anything suspicious, have you? Anything out of the ordinary?"

"No," Mike shook his head. "What's happening, Officer?"

" 'Fraid I can't say. Where are you headed?"

"Mountain Park Campgrounds," Beth said, leaning across Mike to peer up at the policeman. "Up Highway 14."

"Sorry, kids, the 14's off-limits until further notice. For your own safety."

"But *why*?" Beth asked.

"That information is classified. I strongly suggest you get off at the next exit, turn around and go back down the mountain as fast as you can. Keep your windows closed, doors locked and your radio on. Now get out of here!" He thumped the roof of the car with his palm. "*Move on!*" He stepped back from the car and waved us forward with his flashlight.

Mike drove forward and the car quickly picked up speed as the traffic spread out over three lanes.

"You guys, I am so freaking out right now," Beth said, reaching for the radio. Again, static filled the car. She flicked it off. "What do we do now? Go back home?"

"No. We've driven all this way, we've got all this camping stuff. It's our last weekend together. *We are going camping,*" Mike said. "Who's with me?"

The rest of us exchanged glances. There was a long pause.

"I know a back road to the campground," Vance said.

"Then we're going," I said.

Beth let out a little moan but didn't say anything.

Mike pressed the automatic-door-lock button on the driver's side door and all of our door locks clicked down around us. He nodded. "Alright, Vance. Where to?"

***

We followed Vance's directions and ended up on a lonely road that wound around the back side of the mountain, where there weren't any houses. It was pitch dark and the rain was coming down really hard. All we could get out of the radio was a high-pitched whine and Beth had given up on trying to find out any more news that way. Of course, it didn't stop her from further interrogating Vance.

"What do you think your dad meant, when he said that no one would believe it?" She twisted around in the front seat and raised her voice so he could hear her over the pounding of the rain.

"For the millionth time, I don't know, Beth. I'm trying to remember. I think he said something about..." Vance hesitated. "Well, about a crash site. But he sounded excited about it, almost like it was a good thing."

"You guys, I hate to mention this," Mike interrupted, "but I'm getting low on gas. The indicator light just came on. How far are we to the campsite?" He glanced at Vance in the rear view mirror.

Vance frowned out the window. "Have we passed that big rock with the tree growing out of the middle of it?"

"You're kidding me. Vance, I can't see *anything* out there," Mike said.

I stared at Vance. "You don't know where we are, do you? We're lost." A tiny frisson of fear ran up my back and I shivered. "I'm cold and I'm tired and I'm hungry and there's some escaped criminal out there and *we're lost*. Thanks a lot, Vance!"

"We don't know it's a criminal. It could be anything!" Vance shot back at me.

"Thanks a lot, that makes me feel a *lot* better."

Mike pulled the car to the side of the road and turned the motor off, leaving only the headlights on. "We need a plan before we go any further. But first, I've really got to take a piss. Anybody else?" He looked around.

Beth nodded. "I have to go, too. Will you come with me?" she asked me.

"Oh, fine," I grumbled. I pulled up the hood on my raincoat, grabbed my flashlight and followed her out of the car.

Mike crossed to the opposite side of the road and Beth and I headed toward a clump of trees just out of range of the headlights.

"I'm going behind this tree," Beth pointed in front of us. "Hold my flashlight?"

"Ok." I took the flashlight from her and she disappeared behind the tree. For a few moments, it was just me and the rain and the dark. And it didn't feel like a friendly dark. Gusts of wind shook the trees and made shifting shapes of the blackness. "Almost done, Beth?" I called.

Silence.

"Beth?"

Silence.

"BETH?"

Then suddenly a scream ripped through the air and Beth was scrambling toward me, grabbing my arm and half dragging me back toward the car. We slipped and fell, and my hands met the hard gravel of the wet road. "Get in the car, get in the car," Beth panted in my ear.

We reached the car and flung ourselves inside it. Beth slammed down her door lock. "Let's get out of here!" she cried.

"What? What was it?" My heart raced.

"Let's just go!" Beth said again, pounding on the dashboard.

"We can't. Mike's not back yet," Vance said, staring at us with big eyes.

Beth started to cry. "My back," she said, tugging on her jacket and trying to look over her shoulder at her back. "Something got me."

Suddenly the driver's side door was yanked open and Mike threw himself into the front seat. "What happened? Are you OK?"

"We have to get out of here! There's something out there—it got—my back!" Beth was nearly hysterical.

I leaned forward to look at Beth's back. "There's a huge hole in her jacket. It looks like—" I stopped.

"Just start the car," Beth begged.

"It's OK, baby, we're going, we're going," Mike said, jamming the key into the ignition. He turned the key. Nothing happened. He frowned. Tried again. The headlights flickered briefly. He turned them off and then tried the ignition again. Nothing.

"You guys," I said into the silence. "What has three six-inch fingers and the ability to burn a hole in a raincoat, just by touching it?"

"What is this, some kind of sick riddle? We're freakin' stuck here!" Mike snapped at me.

"It's burned onto her back. I can see her skin."

"What do you mean?" Mike spread his hand against the back of Beth's windbreaker, flattening the material. "Damn," he said in awe. "It's burned right through. No tears or anything, just straight burn. Look at the crisp edges."

"It kind of… glows," Vance said slowly. Sure enough, a pale green light seemed to emanate from a mark on Beth's back. She whimpered.

"It's like she's been branded," I said.

The words were barely out of my mouth before a tremendous howling filled the air and something huge smashed onto the top of the car. Vance and I ducked as the ceiling dented above us. Someone screamed.

Mike fumbled with the ignition, urging the car to life. It spluttered and the ignition caught. He floored it and the car went into a tailspin on the slick road, doing a complete 180 before coming to rest, facing in the opposite direction. And there, gleaming in the headlights was a creature unlike any we'd ever seen before. Easily seven feet tall, and thin, with long, scrawny grey arms and a head like an over-large balloon. I had a quick impression of huge almond-shaped black eyes and three-fingered hands raised against us, before Mike gained control of the car and swerved around it.

Vance grabbed the flashlight and swung around in his seat to see out the rear window, but the road was empty. "Did you see? Did you see?" he croaked. "Damn!"

In front of me, Beth was uncharacteristically quiet. I leaned forward to reassure her. "It's OK, Bethie, we're safe. We're leaving."

"We have to go back," she said dully. "They want me."

We stared at her.

"Mike, the road!" I cried, as we swerved toward a tree at the edge of the road. He quickly corrected and resumed our mad dash down the mountain on the curvy road.

"See what's wrong with Beth," he murmured over his shoulder at us.

I leaned way over the front seat and shook her shoulder, but she was unresponsive, her eyes staring straight ahead.

"Stop the car," she said, in a voice unlike her own. "I have a message. *Stop the car.*"

"Beth, I am *not* stopping the car. But I'll have you off of this mountain as fast as I can," Mike said, sparing a quick glance at her.

Beth began a loud, tuneless humming. "The mark is among you now," she said in a sing-song voice, unlike her own. "You've been chosen. They want you back."

"Beth, stop it! This isn't funny!" I shook her furiously. "I don't like this game!"

But Beth just continued the tuneless humming, then slumped in her seat and closed her eyes.

"I think she's passed out," I said. "What's wrong with her? What the hell was that back there?"

"That base. The secret military base—it's for UFOs," Vance blurted out. "I wasn't supposed to say anything. I could get my Dad in serious trouble—but after what we just saw, it doesn't seem to matter anymore."

We rounded another bend in the road and suddenly a police car came wailing into view and skidded to a halt in front of us. Mike slammed down on the brakes and within seconds a policeman was banging on the window. "What are you doing here?! Get out of here!" he yelled at us.

"Officer, we saw—a thing up there in the road," Mike began.

A shuttered look came over the policeman's face. He leaned his head in and spoke quietly. "Look, whatever you saw, I don't want to know. I'm in deep enough as it is. I suggest you get off this mountain as fast as you can and forget anything you *might* have seen." He emphasized the word "might" as if suggesting we hadn't seen anything.

"I'm almost out of gas."

"There's a service station in about three miles. Can you make it that far?"

"I think so."

"Then go."

***

Beth woke up when we pulled into the gas station to get some gas at the bottom of the mountain. She didn't remember anything, from the handprint on. She seemed astounded that there was a hole in her jacket, and kept assuring us that the mark on her back was a birthmark and that it had been there all her life. We looked at the mark again, and it did look faded and old, like something that had been there for years.

When Beth headed into the mini-mart to get a soda, Mike, Vance and I exchanged puzzled glances. What had happened up there on the mountain?

"If she doesn't remember it, I'm not telling her," Mike said, glancing at Beth. He ran his fingers over the fresh dent—really just a scratch—on the roof of the car.

Vance lit a cigarette and narrowed his eyes at Mike. "You're not doing her any favors. If she's been marked for something, maybe she ought to know."

"Don't be stupid! It could have been a branch or something," I said.

"You were the one who said it was a handprint."

I shrugged. "Well, now I'm not so sure."

"And the thing in the road?"

There was a long silence. "Maybe we didn't see—" I began.

"Just shut up," Vance cut me off. "You know what you saw."

***

And that's the thing: I don't know what happened to Beth in those woods. Maybe she just got frightened by an animal, or a branch in the wind. I could explain that away. But the rest is not so easy.

A few days later, I left for my new job in the city, and the others headed off to college and other adventures. We never spoke of that night again. I don't know about the others, but I like to avoid back roads these days. It's as if the policeman's warning lingers in my ears, and behind that a voice says, in a sing-song soft and low, "*They want you back...*"

SNICKERS

By Kelly Reno

Sure, we've all heard plenty of scary stories about a madman with wild eyes, roaming around in the woods looking for his next victim. You know, the typical stories and recycled urban legends you hear while sitting around the campfire roasting marshmallows—how the madman's been out in the woods for so long that his hair is matted and you can smell the rotting stench of his breath just before he attacks you in your sleep.

But I'm certain you've never heard my story before. It happened not too far from here, in fact, it was just over on the next ridge. It wasn't so long ago either.

If you think you've heard this one, trust me, you haven't. If you had, you definitely wouldn't be out in the woods right now with only a nylon tent between you and that Snickers bar you're hiding in your backpack. Sure, you've seen the signs posted around here warning you that your food is supposed to be stowed away in the metal bear boxes. But a Snickers bar isn't really food, you figured. Am I right?

By the way, they say that a bear's favorite food is the Snickers bar and that a bear would do just about *anything* to sink his teeth into one. But bears are the last thing you need to worry about around here…

Look, I'm not trying to freak you out or anything. I just think that you should know the facts because the authorities did their best to cover up the whole incident. I mean, with a madman running loose in the woods, who would come camping up here? Nobody would—because he was never captured. But I know the truth about what happened—*I know because I was there.*

I was up here with my best friend and we were just getting settled in our tent for the night. Even though it was the middle of summer, it was kind of chilly outside, so I took a flashlight and unlocked my friend's car and I was digging around in the backseat for my sweatshirt. I finally found it and pulled it over my head, then sat back in the seat to warm up before I trekked across the clearing over to the tent. We'd been hiking all day and I was really tired and my stomach was rumbling with hunger. But I was so exhausted that I fell asleep in the car.

I awoke in the middle of the night with the light of the full moon shining in my eyes through the windshield. I stepped outside to stretch my cramped limbs and was considering sleeping in the car, but then I smelled it, the unmistakable tang of it filling my nostrils. My heart began to thud violently within my chest because I knew that it could only be *one thing.* There was a madman lurking around!

Against my better judgment, I found myself barreling toward the campsite. It was pretty foggy out that night, but I remember seeing the dim light within the tent and the silhouette of my buddy through the thin, nylon shelter. I heard him groaning and I heard ripping, then I heard the sickening crunch from within the tent, a sound that made my blood run cold. My palms began to sweat with panic. The flashlight slipped from my hands and clattered to the ground.

Stumbling blindly through the darkness, I remember crashing into the tent and then I heard it—*a bloodcurdling scream coming from my own throat.*

After that things went fuzzy and I must have blacked out from the horror of what I'd seen that night. Before everything went black, I remember the sight of the tent shaking violently just before it collapsed.

The next morning, I found myself alone and buried beneath the collapsed remains of the tent. The car was long gone and so was my best friend. He must've run for his own life and left me behind. I never heard from him again.

The authorities came to check out the campsite. Unsure of what they were dealing with, they told me to keep quiet and they reported the incident in their log book as a wild animal attack. But there was no trace of a wild animal anywhere, not even a set of footprints, just a trampled tent and the scattered remains of our campsite.

But I knew the truth because I was there... I kept my mouth shut about what happened that night—*until now...*

HE NEVER SHOULD HAVE EATEN MY SNICKERS BAR!

The Ghost Camper
By Barbara Oliver

A TRUE STORY!

Our campsite was nestled in the wooded hills of southern Indiana near a lake where we often went swimming during our one-week camping trip. Our site had a number of other groups staying there and we were all in four-man canvas tents which were mounted on a raised wooden platform.

We always hung our wet bathing suits out to dry on a line run between two trees about thirty feet from our tent. We began to notice a curious happening—every morning our bathing suits were off the line and trampled in the mud on the ground underneath. We wondered what this could be—animals? Angry neighbors? It happened several days in a row and we were dumbfounded.

***

One night, after this had happened four days in a row, I was settling down to go to sleep in the tent with the back door flap open to let in some night breeze. I heard leaves crunching underfoot in the trees behind the tent. Crunch, crunch, they went, with every footstep. I peered out into the darkness and could make out a dark figure near our bathing suit line. I watched as the figure appeared to pause and become quiet near the trees where our suits were hung. I thought, "Could this be the intruder we have wondered about?"

After a few moments the dark figure began to move again, and the crunch of the leaves underfoot began again. Crunch, crunch in the leaves, the figure slowly was moving toward our tent! I could begin to make out some detail in the dim moonlight. It was a young girl! She was walking directly toward me and I called out, "Hello! Hello!" but there was no answer.

She walked forward as if I had said nothing and was not there. She came so close I could make out the details of her clothes, a dirty white shirt, shorts and two mismatched socks above her sneakers.

She appeared to stare straight ahead as if she were a zombie and I called out again, "Hello! Hello!" louder and louder but it did no good. By now I was terrified, as she was only feet from me. I froze in terror as she stepped up onto my tent platform and walked to the side of my bunk. But she didn't stop. Still staring straight ahead as if hypnotized, she walked straight through my body! As I turned my head, I saw her pass right through the canvas side of the tent, and then the sounds of footsteps crunching in the forest leaves continued as she walked away through the forest.

Needless to say, I hardly got a wink of sleep for the rest of the night. I had seen a ghost!

Two days later, as we loaded our gear into the car for the trip home, a young girl across the parking lot caught my eye. I looked closer and saw the same girl, the same dirty white shirt, shorts and mismatched socks. But this was no ghost—it was one of the campers leaving the site with her family!

The Howling
By Barbara Bowman

Jessica unpacked the back of her Volvo station wagon and carried bags of groceries to a small shack with moss-covered shingles in the woods. Her black lab, Russ, was running about in excitement over his new environment. Jessica had decided to take a break from Seattle and get some R & R in the backwoods of the Olympic Peninsula, far from the buzz of urban life. She had a book deadline approaching and she needed time away from the city to complete it. Deep in the woods, there was not a human for miles around, just what she needed to give her space to write. Jessica paused briefly on her front porch and inhaled deeply, the air fragrant with earth and trees.

Before she delved into her writing, Jessica decided to make a delicious dinner to begin her week-long stay. She had brought some root vegetables like parsnips, turnips, and carrots, which she chopped and combined with cubes of red meat in a kettle on the fire. The smell was fantastic. Russ's salivation was dripping to the floor as he watched her. Jessica finalized the prep for the stew and sat down to write on her typewriter as the stew simmered to a perfectly thick, rich flavor. The words streamed out of her, as if a floodgate had been opened. Russ lay on the floor beside her, occasionally looking over at the kettle on the fire and licking his lips. Jessica made some good headway into her writing, and before she knew it, the stew was ready for eating. The sun had completely set, leaving the fire and a candle the only light in the cabin. Everything was perfect.

Jessica settled into the rocking chair by the fire with her dinner, when Russ started to growl under his breath. Jessica tried to quiet him, but he continued growling and paced around the room, completely ignoring his large bowl of stew. Russ was clearly bothered by something outside of the cabin. Jessica figured it was a deer or something Russ wanted to chase, but Russ seemed more upset and riled than eager for the hunt. Just then, something howled in the distance, breaking the silence of the night. *Could it be a coyote? It must be*, thought Jessica. *Coyotes are common in this part of the country*. Because there was no moon out the outside was as black as ink, which made it impossible to see anything, even right in front of your face.

But then, there was another howl, only this time closer. It sounded like a coyote but with more desperation, and lower-pitched. Jessica started to get scared, her heart beating faster, her breathing getting heavier. Her body had definitely kicked into fight-or-flight in full effect. Russ started barking wildly, with the hair on his back standing up on end. Jessica had never seen him like this before.

Just then, Jessica heard a crack outside, like when one steps on a fallen branch. By this point, Russ was going crazy, his barks almost roar-like in their intensity and ferociousness. He jumped up on the door, scratching to get out. Jessica looked fervently around the cabin for something to use as a weapon. But there wasn't much, only a few logs for the fire and her rocking chair. The howling began again, but this time it was right outside. Jessica's body was covered with goose bumps. She had never heard a howl so frightening in all of her life. But then she remembered her knife for cooking and grabbed it, making a white-knuckled fist.

The bottom step of the front porch creaked as something stepped on it. Russ was about ready to jump through the window, and Jessica's body was on high alert. Everything was brighter, and every little sound was amplified, as if her senses had multiplied in strength.

Another creak came from something stepping on the porch right outside the door. Jessica gripped the knife with everything she had, heart about ready to explode, her body shaking with every beat. The door knob turned slowly… slowly… Then, the door swung open making a loud bang as it hit the wall. Jessica stared in disbelief, as did Russ. Standing before them was something that has only been captured on film a few times.

It was—Bigfoot!

In a mousy voice, he said, "I hope you don't mind the intrusion, but I wanted to welcome you to the neighborhood. I am starving for something new to eat around here and was hoping you wouldn't mind sharing your dinner. I brought some delicious mushrooms I found, and we could share or something." Both Jessica and Russ passed out on the floor. Being careful not to hit his head on the ceiling, Bigfoot made his way to the food and dug in. "Suit yourself," he said with a shrug and made himself comfortable.

A Campfire Tale

By Garett Martell

A TRUE STORY!

After waiting for what seemed like an eternity, I was finally a teenager. I made it through freshman year in middle school with my self-esteem mostly intact, but becoming a teenager appeared to be more about responsibilities than the rights I had envisioned.

I wanted to show the world I was no longer a kid. I had worked hard on my paper route the year before and thought it was about time I bought myself a new ten-speed and a bookshelf-type record player with two-way detachable speakers. I was the envy of my friends who had always been too busy to work. We often stayed up listening to my records. *Bat Out of Hell* came out that year and we wore it out. We wore out my mom, too.

Middle school finished earlier than other schools in my city by a little over a week. My mother had been dying to get out to our beach cottage and was intent on dragging this less-than-enthusiastic teenager with her. After all, I had all sorts of things to do now, and being stuck at the lake with the family was not my idea of fun.

My mom let me take a friend along. Robert had been there several times before over the last few years and she liked him, so that was easy. We spent the first week fishing and swimming every day. Nights were for building a campfire or playing chess.

Robert and I walked to the store and talked about having our own adventure. We imagined canoeing down the river all the way to the ocean, going hiking along the trails that seemed to head to the end of the earth and a dozen other crazy things that popped into our teenaged heads. We laughed as we walked, licking our ice cream.

"Why don't we go camping?" I blurted out and took another lick while waiting for an answer.

"Where?" asked Robert as he tried to catch the ice cream running down his fingers.

I chuckled and watched him desperately trying to get it all as it continued to melt.

"There's a place close to the lake," I offered.

Robert finally made headway on his licking and was able to answer. "Ever camped there?" he muttered between licks.

"No. I used to pass it when my mom dropped me off at the pier to go fishing."

Robert nodded in agreement.

"There won't be many people here for another week. We could get the spot closest to the lake," I enthusiastically added.

Losing ground again on the ice cream, Robert finally shoved it all in his mouth. I laughed and we continued walking.

My mom was a little hesitant about having us go off camping by ourselves, but this was probably the safest place in the country and it was at a time and place far removed from the insanity that seems to go on in the world today.

We dug out the camping gear that hadn't been used for a few years, dusted it off and loaded up.

***

We had lots of choices for where to pitch the tent. It was the middle of the week and school was still on for most kids. The lifeguard chair at the lake was empty since they didn't start until the next week but that didn't stop us. We set up the tent then headed off to the beach.

When we went back to the tent, we noticed someone else had arrived a few spots away. We could see the tent through the bushes in the distance but didn't see anyone.

We changed into dry clothes and rummaged through the food bag looking for something to eat. I pulled out buns and wieners and we both looked at the fire pit.

"I'll look for firewood," offered Robert.

"I'll get water," I said.

There was a faucet sticking out of the ground not far away. I grabbed the jug and headed over as Robert headed off toward the bushes and returned shortly.

I looked at the small armful of firewood he had. "We'll need more than that."

"This was all I could find," said Robert apologetically.

"There used to be some in the racks down by the showers. If we both go, we can get a lot."

Robert nodded and we headed off toward the showers. We walked and talked, laughing much of the time. Finally reaching the racks, we saw that there was a little weathered wood left from last year. We started filling our arms when we heard something inside the showers.

We looked at each other and agreed that it had come from inside. Startled, we stood there with our arms full of wood, waiting. Then we heard giggles. We were puzzled, but a little relieved.

WHAM! The door flew open and hit the garbage can. Out came two girls, a few years older than us, wrapped in towels and carrying their bikinis.

We were shocked. Robert dropped his wood, which startled them, and one shrieked.

We all stood there for a silent moment waiting for someone to break the silence.

The girls giggled and we all started to lighten up a bit.

Trying to sound mature beyond my years, I spoke up.

"Uh… Hi," I said in the coolest way I could muster.

Tracy and Jackie, as we later learned their names were, giggled again.

"We thought we were all alone," Tracy informed us.

"Us too," Robert said.

They looked at the wood we'd gathered, then over at the woodpile. There were only a few scraps we hadn't got to yet. "We were looking for wood too," Tracy informed us.

Almost embarrassed at this point, we stood there trying to think of something cool to say. I started to fidget and Tracy spoke up.

"Doesn't look like there's enough for two fires," Jackie said.

"Uh… no," I responded awkwardly.

"Why don't we have a fire together?" she fished.

"Sure," Robert blurted almost before the words came from her mouth.

"Okay. We are just down the end of the road by the lake," Tracy said, as she pointed away from where our site was.

Wanting desperately to let them know we were by ourselves, I boasted, "My mom dropped us off down the other end."

Tracy smiled.

"We're on our own," I added, trying not to sound too stupid.

"Us too. Our dad had to run back to the city."

Jackie cut in, "We'll change and be down later."

"Okay," Robert and I chorused together.

They took off, looking back a couple times, giggling as they walked. We tore our gaze away so we wouldn't look ridiculous and started gathering every scrap of wood we could find.

***

It was getting dark and the fire started to roar. The girls walked up and seemed to glow in the firelight. It was a little awkward since we didn't know what to do with girls and they were teasing us for their own amusement. I dished out the hot dogs, trying to focus on something I could actually do. Nervously, Robert added more wood to the fire. We sat and watched as we cooked, and talked a bit as we ate.

After her last bite, Jackie leaned forward. "I know what we can do."

Robert and I sat anxiously, waiting for her to finish.

"We can tell scary stories," she continued.

Tracy got quite excited. "Yeah!" They both looked at us, waiting for a reply.

A little disappointed, but at the same time totally relieved, I gulped and smiled. Robert loved the idea and moved closer to Jackie.

We listened intently as Jackie told her story. Robert seemed to hang on her every word and motion as she tried to be as scary as she could. It wasn't scary but we went along eagerly as she continued. She finished and we realistically faked enough interest, I think, that she was satisfied.

Tracy told the next one and I really was interested as she sat closer to me than before. It was a better story so there wasn't as much faking.

Then it was my turn. I had a couple from Scout camp that I remembered and tried to think of the best one.

"Come on," urged Tracy, "make it scary."

I thought again for a moment.

"I know a couple scary stories, but I have a true story that's much scarier."

"I love those," Jackie said. Tracy nodded as they prodded me to continue.

"Well," I began, as the girls moved closer in anticipation. "It's about campers up north." Their eyes widened in enthusiasm.

"It's a remote campsite, far off the roads that was abandoned by the parks board years before. The sites are mostly overgrown now. There were never any showers that far off the road and the outhouses, now badly weathered, are not much better than picking the nearest tree."

They were becoming hooked.

"Seldom did anyone venture back that far. It wasn't on the maps anymore and the only road in from the highway had old beaten-up signs trying to discourage people from using it. 'Closed,' they all said. But the hardcore campers never cared. Some saw more of an adventure and others just wanted to get away. No one is sure how or when it got started, but we know how it ended."

They were really hooked now.

"The brother of a young married couple in Calgary came to visit them with his girlfriend. They decided to go camping and wanted to 'get back to nature,' so they headed off to this place. They were there through the first day, swimming and sitting around the fire at night. As the darkest part of the night fell and they lay sound asleep, feet rustled through the long grass in the distance. In the morning they all got up, had breakfast and sat around drinking the first coffee of the day. The husband walked over to his truck and started looking for something. Puzzled, he came back and asked if anyone had seen his axe. No one had, and he looked around his gear.

"After dinner the brother and girlfriend took the canoe as the man and wife hung out on shore. The air was still, like a vacuum, and the canoe cut through the water to the far side of the lake. Back on shore, the man and wife put on some music and relaxed by the fire. The water rippled as something big entered from shore. A man's arm held an axe just above the water. The ripples continued as he walked slowly through the water. He worked his way through tall weeds along the shore to get nearer the canoe and slowly dropped down into the water. He swam quietly over to the canoe, grabbed the side and flipped it, dumping the unaware couple into the water. He thrashed around with the axe, hacking and slashing at the couple until there was no more movement and the water was left a chilling red. A cap floated nearby."

This was working out better than I had hoped. Tracy was holding my arm tight and Jackie had taken off her coat and was cozying up to Robert.

"The man and wife slowly arose as dusk fell. The wife looked out over the water as the husband put more wood on the fire. 'I don't see any sign of them,' she said. 'Well, they'll be able to find their way by firelight,' he said, trying to reassure her, although he was a little worried himself. 'Do you think they are okay?' she queried. 'Hey, Jimmy can handle himself. Just relax; I'm sure they'll be back soon,' her husband told her. Still worried, she nodded and set about getting dinner ready. Trying to keep busy as the skies darkened, she started heating water on the fire. Needing tea, she headed back to the truck.

"The man was looking out over the lake when he heard a thud. Thinking she must have dropped the water jug, he headed over to help. It was quite dark now, and when he got to the truck he saw her slumped over the back. He shook her and called out her name, but she didn't respond. He turned on his flashlight, shined it on her, and then recoiled in shock at the sight of her nearly severed head. He fell backwards and stumbled back to his feet, spinning around frantically. The killer stood before him, holding his blood-stained axe. The husband was helplessly in shock as the axe rose and fell on his body, again and again until he hit the ground and stopped moving."

The girls seemed genuinely scared as I emphasized some of the gory parts. Robert was also a little quieter than I expected.

"They finally caught the guy, tried him and put him away for murder. He got twenty-five years and is supposed to be getting out of the pen soon."

The eyes of the girls widened.

"That's right, Stoney Mountain, barely five miles from this very spot."

By this time they were totally focused on the story, waiting expectantly for the rest.

"I'm sure you've heard the news. Percy Mogey is getting released soon, maybe already has," I continued enthusiastically.

The girls jolted back at the words. Robert was a little startled as well. It was a little more reaction than I had expected but I was enthused at having them hanging on my every word. But the girls seemed to go into shock as I continued on with my story. I knew I could probably tell them more, since my Grandfather had been a guard at the pen and had a few run-ins with Percy Mogey over the years. I decided to add a little more.

"It just so happens that I have a personal connection to Percy."

The girls started crying and hugged each other as they moved away from us. Confused, Robert looked at me as I tried to figure out what had happened.

"Are you okay?" I asked the girls.

"You're a jerk." Tracy's words cut through me like a knife.

Someone was walking up to our site. There was so much anger from the girls, we didn't notice the rustling footsteps.

"Percy Mogey was our Grandfather!" an angry Jackie added.

I recoiled in horror at what I had done. Robert sat there in total disbelief. It seemed like an eternity had passed, then a figure suddenly appeared before us in the glow of the fire—a tall, hulking giant of a man. He stopped between us and the girls, towering over us all. He looked at the girls and then at us, in silence. We wanted to run but couldn't get our feet to move. We had forgotten all about the girls as he looked at us, and we didn't notice them get to their feet until they stepped over to greet him, crying as they sought comfort. Robert and I sat there, too afraid to move, trying to figure out what was happening and just waiting helplessly for whatever was going to happen next.

They spoke to him quietly, with his back turned to us. He looked over his shoulder—for the first time we could see his weathered face. It surely looked like the face of a killer.

It was Percy's son—their dad.

He stepped over to us and stopped. His silence was deafening. The only thing we heard was the beating of our hearts, which seemed to drown out the crackle of the fire and everything else. He must have heard it too. He looked at me and then Robert as he stepped over between us and bent over.

Oh, no. This is the end. I don't want to die like this!

He reached down, grabbing Jackie's coat that lay on the log and then stood back up. He gave us a really disgusted gaze, stepped back and then put his arms around the girls, huddling them off to their site.

***

Robert and I spent the entire night awake in our tents, shivering and waiting for death to pay us a visit. Every rustle of the leaves set us to trembling more. At the first crack of daylight, we hurriedly packed up all our stuff and walked all the way back to the cottage. We never spoke to anyone about this, including each other.

The Mill

By Corinne Simon-Duneau

Most of the boys had arrived that morning. There weren't any uniforms. This was going to be an informal affair. The school was, as always on Easter break, not officially functioning, but had stayed partly open for the traditional Lakewood Initiation. Some of the children were wearing corduroys, some jeans. They were still too young to be wearing anything too fashionable or showy. Most had parkas against the chill. Some had sweaters underneath, not the kind they would buy themselves, but lovingly chosen by cautious mothers.

The trees were still bare, some had tiny buds appearing. The air was pure and maybe a little humid. Their breaths made little puffs of mist as they walked up the driveway, just back from their after-dinner walk around the lake. The dean had invited all fifteen of them to his house. He was to brief and orient them on the next days' activities and the initiation to come.

As they sat around in the library, some on the couches and armchairs, some on the Persian rug by the fireplace, warm tea and chocolate were brought along with the promised, special homemade cookies.

The dean introduced himself and welcomed the boys. "You have been hand-picked," he said, "among the brightest boys in the country to spend a week here. You'll be instructed on various subjects before you continue your schooling. Soon, it will be time for you to go to college. You may come back after that. I'd be happy if you did. However, why wait until you're a man to start learning about what it is to be a man? You all know it's an honor to be invited to participate in the

Lakewood Initiation. But I'm also honored to have you here, as you are the future elite of this country."

He took a sip of brandy—he was the only adult around, except the maid who had disappeared—and put his glass back on the mantelpiece. He took a long breath, with his head down, as if meditating on what he was going to say. He put both hands behind his back and continued, "However, I would be remiss if I didn't tell you something you need to know about this school and the Lakewood Initiation. Many years ago…"

And this is the story he told them:

A group of children had arrived in the morning for the Lakewood Initiation on a chilly early spring day. That very night, they received a briefing about the initiation. It would take place the next night and they had to be warmly dressed. They would also need flashlights even though the moon was full and you could see almost as clearly as in daylight. But it would be dark in the mill.

They had been preparing and drilling all afternoon and had left just after dark. They walked in a group, rather subdued by now, even though they had been chatty and excited during dinner, which had been particularly good—roast beef and mashed potatoes with gravy and green beans and a great cake with ice cream on top.

The teacher and his younger assistant were walking ahead, fast, and talking in hushed low tones. The children found it comforting to hear them chuckle once or twice. Was the mill really haunted? The teacher had seemed serious about it. He had given them strict instructions to follow, lest they derange the mill's ghost and risk injury or worse. It was, after all, an initiation. But if they obeyed the rules, they would be safe. It was the best way to become adults; learn to master their fears and keep their nerve.

They reached a forest, climbed up through it and then went down into a deep, narrow valley. By the time they arrived at the mill, it was almost eight o'clock and they were beat. They stood by a dark river with a strong current. The moonlight wasn't as bright as it was earlier in the plain surrounding the school. The grove was thick and huge rocks loomed on the other side of the river. Half the mill had gone to ruin but the other half still stood somewhat, and the big wooden wheel was there too, although green with moss and algae hanging from the axle. There was a gigantic brick chimney against the side of the stone building. It soared, even above the highest trees, and was surprisingly intact compared to the rest of the mill. In the night, it looked lighter in color, newer, or as if someone had brushed it clean.

The teacher stopped and beckoned them closer. They all gathered around him. He lifted his hand to command silence, although no one was speaking much. "From the moment we start the initiation," he said quietly, "no one is to utter a word. If you absolutely have to, then it should be in the lowest voice possible. Speaking aloud, screaming or other loud noise can have grave repercussions. Better be safe and stay silent."

Someone attempted a dumb joke about what happened if you needed to burp, but apart from a suppressed chuckle or two, he was ignored.

"The most important thing to remember," the teacher said, "is *never*, under *any* circumstance or for *any* reason, *touch* the chimney or approach it closer than six feet. This is 'his', or maybe even 'he', and he's been keeping it 'alive' in a way. And he *is* dangerous, I cannot stress this enough. I repeat, a wrong move can have *dire* consequences, for you and your fellow initiates." The teacher paused for a few seconds, letting his words enter the young minds in his care. He looked solemn as he continued. "I want all of you to assess whether you feel you want to go ahead with this and take responsibility for your own actions and those of your fellow initiates. If not, it's perfectly all right and you won't be penalized for it in any way. Being an adult is also knowing your limits and not making promises you cannot keep. You have three minutes to think it over."

The children all looked at the chimney with dread. It seemed to glow in the dark, maybe the product of their imagination. It did have an ethereal appearance though; it was a bit transparent, as if a projected image rather than a solid brick structure.

None of them opted out, although most felt like doing so.

It had seemed easy enough when the teacher had briefed them: go inside one by one, find the kiln room. The kiln room was a stone lean-to built around the base of the chimney, so its brick wall would be visible. Inside, there would be vestiges of the large brick oven around an opening in the chimney. You weren't to approach the chimney itself. Just get one brick from the oven and bring it back out, at which time the next initiate would be behind you to do the same. They would be leaving at fifteen-minute intervals and there should never be more than one person at a time in the kiln room. Fifteen minutes was plenty of time to get there, so if you arrived at the entrance of the kiln room too early you had to wait in another room. You were to be very careful not to fall, bump into anything, drop anything or generally make any noise whatsoever.

Now the task seemed daunting. What if someone did trip? It could have grave consequences for all of them, he had said. You had to count not only on yourself but also on others to not mess up. This was to be more an act of faith in your mates than of courage. But they held fast. Their honor was at stake, too.

"And remember," the teacher repeated, "no noise. Even burping." He was not smiling; he was looking at the author of the earlier remark, who was trying to dig a hole in the ground with the tip of his shoe. "I want you to understand that this is not a joke, or a game. It's deadly serious."

As the night wore on, they went in, one by one. It was, actually, nerve-racking.

***

The dean took a log and added it to the fire. He poked the embers for a few seconds. The log spit little sparks on the rug and he placed a screen in front of the fireplace. The children, who had been listening without a sound, shifted a bit and took some cookies from the plates in front of them.

"Of three young initiates," he said, "two were able to give sketchy accounts of their initiation at the mill. One of them, however—I can't give you his name—agreed to give a full description of what he went through and fortunately, he was recorded. It seemed to corroborate the others' accounts but was remarkably detailed. Much later, I listened to it many times, trying to understand what had happened and why. I know it almost by heart."

***

He entered through the ruined part of the mill. At first, he had to weave his way through collapsed roofs and beams, a landmine zone of broken tiles that cracked under his feet and squeaking wooden floors—did that count as a noise? He stopped and listened, his heart racing, his legs weak. Then he reached the part that was still standing. He went through a metal door, down a few damp steps, into a dark room. He could hear water dripping, the river close behind the wall.

As he walked further into the room, it became pitch dark. The flashlight was inadequate. It only lit a yard, maybe two, in front of him. There was no way of seeing how big the room was or how far he had to go. He couldn't help imagining, *feeling* that something in there was lurking, observing him. The floor was wet; it smelled of decomposing algae and was slippery. It was hard to keep his balance because his legs were shaking. At least it was made of flagstones, not decayed, worm-eaten wood, so he felt he had a better chance of staying on course.

Then there was the *existing* noise. Creaking rafters, wind picking up and moving things somewhere. Scratching, rasping sounds, things scurrying suddenly next to him, and he had to will himself not to jump. He kept thinking encouraging thoughts, obsessively, and he knew that was a bit strange but he had to: *it must be just mice, or simply birds, or branches ruffling.* He forced himself to smile, to make fun of himself: *look at you, like a girl, afraid of mice. Just because the teacher said there was a ghost, you're becoming a wimp?*

But he couldn't help worrying anyway: if *someone else* made noise, if a bird knocked something, would it affect "*him*", the chimney, or whatever it was? God, how he wished he had thought of these questions before he had set out. But worst of all were the things that suddenly touched him, or crawled on him. He didn't even know what he was imagining or what was real. He couldn't stop either because he was being timed. So he had to let whatever was brushing his arm brush his arm, grit his teeth and hope for the best.

Now he had to find the oven. It seemed he had been gone forever and he could not find the oven. Was this the kiln room? He couldn't *see* anything. He didn't know where he was. Was he walking around in circles? A cold sweat appeared on his hands. His skin prickled. His heart felt like it was shrinking. He knew he needed to get a hold of himself and not be a fool. It couldn't be that difficult to find his way. Just keep going. He did keep going but couldn't see an opening anywhere, either in front, or behind him. He couldn't see the metal door.

So he started thinking encouraging thoughts again. But it didn't really work. His mouth was dry, his chest hurt and his throat trembled. This was stupid, suicidal—why on earth had he volunteered? He was lost. He'd screwed up. They would have to come for him. Maybe he was trapped. He felt he had entered a parallel world and would never go home again. He longed for home. He thought of his mom and dad and what an idiot he'd been for not wanting to be with them at times. Now it seemed like paradise. His bedroom, his bed, his familiar stuff. He wanted to cry; he wanted out. This was supposed to make you grow up?

And suddenly he saw it: a short ladder in a recess, looking innocent and pure, and it led to a weak light. He was so happy he wanted to kiss it, but was careful not to hurry too much. Up he went, into a tunnel, through an arch and there it was—a smaller room, with windows. There was enough moonlight to see, at the end of it, a crumbled oven.

He stopped and looked at the back wall. It was entirely made of brick and he knew that was "*it*", the chimney. It bulged and had a big, dark opening into it, like a gaping mouth. Was it moving? Breathing? It looked like it was, but then several things looked like they were moving. It was his eyes. He was tired. There was a big pile of bricks in front of the oven. He wasn't really breathing himself, so he had to take a deep gulp of moldy air and tell himself to calm down. *It's almost over. It should be easy—before making any further move, take your bearings. The teacher said no closer than six feet from the chimney. Choose your brick at a safe distance from the chimney.* Straining his eyes to see if any obstacle was in the way, he examined the floor in front of him and started moving...

***

Then, he forgot how he had gotten out. He vaguely remembered making a beeline for the brick and taking it, that his ears were ringing, or he was hearing bells. All he knew was that he had his brick in his hand. Miraculously, he found the way out, through some opening in the wall. Did he really go down a few steps? Did he bump into anything? Did he make any noise? He didn't remember. He just went out, almost flew out, and recalled feeling the fresh air hit him, filling his lungs, bringing him back to life.

All he had to do now was go around the mill. The path was dark but it was outside, he was outside! He ran, he was running away from the chimney, and he recognized the clearing where the others were. And then he saw them.

Suddenly, he fought back tears of relief and forced a ridiculously stretched grin, hoping nobody would read him in the dark. They were all there, waiting for him—minus the one who had gone after him. He wanted to wave his brick in the air with pride, as the others had, except he didn't. He was shaking so much he thought he might not have the strength to lift his arm. Also, he didn't feel so proud.

He hadn't paid attention to those who had gone before him, because they hadn't seemed frightened. Now he wondered. Because the ones who had not gone yet were looking at him with envy, and anxious, questioning eyes. He wouldn't talk, because he knew his voice might waver, or he might burst into tears. So he just gave them a thumbs-up, mouthing "piece of cake" with that stupid grimace plastered on his face.

He stood there, slowly waking from a bad dream. Was he betraying them? No, he'd just been a dingbat. Telling them anything would be a betrayal. There was no ghost, and it was indeed a rite of passage and a hard lesson learned. So let them go through it too, since there was no danger other than a bruise, a spider bite or a good fright. The rest of them went in, one after the other, and each came out with his brick, some looking more shaken than others. Everybody was exhausted, it was nearly midnight. But it would soon be over and they'd all go to bed and talk about it the next day. It would be interesting to see who would tell the truth.

Finally, only one was left to go. Two were in. One of them should be coming out anytime now.

Except he didn't.

And the other one didn't either.

It was over twenty-five minutes now. The kids huddled and started talking, in hushed voices. What worried them most was that the teacher and his assistant had looked at each other and seemed worried too—more than worried. The teacher leaned towards the assistant and talked into his ear. The assistant nodded and the teacher turned to the children and said, "Wait here, we'll be right back." Leaving the uneasy boys by themselves, they started towards the mill at a hurried pace.

Then they heard the scream.

It shot into them and paralyzed them like a poisoned arrow. It was all the terror and the pain in the world in one single, long howl that never seemed to end. Some children started running away in the direction of the school; some couldn't move, petrified; and some, the bravest, ran toward the mill, shouting at each other, oblivious of the warnings, oblivious of the chimney. They ran right past it and went inside. Those that did go regretted it forever.

They came upon a scene of horror. It was far more horrible than horror in horror movies because it was so real—and so unnecessary. One of them, one of their *friends*, was pounding at the other kid, his best pal, with a brick, going, "Huh! Huh! Huh!" in his frantic efforts. The teacher pulled him off his victim but he struggled to continue. His eyes were haggard, his mouth wide open in a silent scream and he drooled. He breathed fast and talked incoherently. The assistant held the other child in his arms. He had a nasty gash on the head. He was unconscious and covered in blood, his hair sticky and red.

***

The children gasped. Up to then, they had been deliciously scared by the dean's tale, confident it would all end well. This was unexpected—almost a letdown.

"Did he survive?" asked one of the children. "What happened; how come he was beating the other one up?"

"To answer the first question, yes, he did survive. Barely," said the dean. "But he made it."

They sighed, relieved.

"As for the second question, here is what seems to have happened, but nobody is certain. The initiate who had been there first had taken his brick and was about to leave, when the boy who had left after him—the youngest of all, by the way—suddenly appeared, unexpectedly, from another entrance. The little one hadn't waited in another room because he was frightened and wanted to be with his friend. We think the older one was so startled that he lost it. He may have hallucinated, and thought he was attacked by some ghoul."

The children gasped again, appalled.

The dean nodded sadly and continued: "Unfortunately, the story doesn't end here."

Was this for real or was he just fooling them and keeping them on their toes? He certainly didn't look like he was kidding. They were smart enough to know he might be pulling their leg. Nevertheless, they kept a respectful silence. The dean was sipping his brandy, gazing at the flames with a somber expression on his face.

"The kid who attacked his friend never stopped seeing ghouls. He went mad."

"Oh no!" someone cried.

Now they were really wondering. If it was a joke, it was not funny; it was tasteless. If it wasn't a joke, then it certainly didn't make them feel like being there.

"We're not going to go to the mill for our initiation, are we?" said an apprehensive little voice, as thin as a shepherd's flute.

"No, certainly not," said the dean brusquely. "We've never been back there, of course. And for more reasons than one."

This was starting to get scary. It *was* for real. Or was it? They waited.

"One year later, the kid that was beaten up went mad too…"

Their silence became tangible. Almost thick.

"Sadly, it was the anniversary…"

He paused, and started walking back and forth. He looked like he was in pain. He wasn't making any effort to hide his feelings and this was deeply troubling to his audience. Some of them wanted to leave, go home, now. But they didn't want to look afraid so they displayed ironic smiles, as if they knew what was coming. "In fact," the dean continued, "of the fifteen children who were there, fourteen had picked up a brick, and…" He brought his fingers to his brow and rubbed it. There was a slight tremor to his lips. Was he going to *cry*? "And all of them went mad," he said, "each year, one after the other." They strained to hear him. "Then the teacher too, and his assistant. All sixteen of them, lost in an insane world of terror. And the terrible thing is, it always happened at the anniversary."

That's what made some of them suspect it was a prank. The bit about the anniversary. Straight out of the lamest horror flick. How about the tearing up though? And the shaking fingers? Would he fake that?

"The last one," the dean said, "the one who never got a chance to go in…" He hesitated. He had paled.

"What happened to him?" someone asked.

"It was I."

There was a silence as the children looked at him, incredulous.

"You?"

"That was you? You're kidding, right?"

Some of them had gotten up, ready to bolt for the door. Some watched him, thinking, here comes the punch line, now he's going to laugh. But he didn't laugh.

"So… What happened to you?"

"I'm glad you asked," he said with a half-smile. This was a bit reassuring for the most nervous ones and they all watched him closely now. "Well, it's been thirty years since the last one went… lost his mind. Forty-six anniversaries exactly, and nothing's happened to me. I'm sane as sane can be."

The ones that had gotten up sat back down, embarrassed. The questions erupted in the room.

"How come we never heard about this? It would be known!"

"Come on, it's getting late, tell us the truth."

"Is this a joke or what?"

"When did it happen?"

"Did they really go mad?"

"What did their parents say?"

"How come the school is still open?"

"So, did anybody actually *see* a ghost?"

"How far is the mill from here?"

Most of the boys were standing now. They were all speaking at the same time, some sounding irritated, others apprehensive.

The dean held his hand up, shouting, "All right! All right! All right!" until they fell silent again. "I will answer all of these questions in time," he said. "The reason you never heard about it is that no one, or practically no one, ever found out and it was swept under the carpet. I will explain why later, as I think you ought to be informed. But before that, there's one more thing I wanted to tell you…" He finished his brandy, making a little gulping noise, and resumed his pacing. "All these years, one thing stayed on my mind and became more and more important as time went by. And that is, I never went in to get my own brick. This meant I had not undergone the initiation I was entitled to in my own right. Did this make me less of a man? I would never know, would I? All my life, I have felt unqualified, incomplete. However, I *always* resisted the temptation to go to the mill and get my brick. Year after year after year, I have yearned to go back. However, I knew better. That's probably why…"

He was slowly walking towards the end of the room. He stopped in front of a mahogany cabinet, opened it and bent down. They couldn't really hear what he was saying. "That's probably why…" he repeated as he got up, his back to them, "I was spared. And today is the anniversary again…"

He turned around. He was holding something in his hands. It was wrapped in green silk. He unwrapped it and held it up. It was a brick. "I was spared!" he screamed, "SPARED! SPARED! SPARED! SPARED! SPAAAAARED!" Then he laughed, louder and louder and louder.

That's when he started running towards them.

The Legend of the Milky Way

By Joanna Celeste

There is a story, whispered among children huddled around a campfire, which tells of how the Milky Way came to be.

Once upon a time, long before there were trees and rivers, planets and stars, or the moons that circled them, there was a thing, dark and plain and full of possibility, called Space.

At that time, there wasn't just one god, or even ten, but millions and millions of them. All these gods had a little section of Space where they could set up their playground and do whatever they wanted.

Since there never seemed to be an end to this Space, the children of the gods—who were gods themselves, but didn't know it yet—asked for a little section, too.

One of these children we will call Infinity.

Infinity had been to the playgrounds of some of the gods and saw that some of their toys—which they called planets—had little people who played around on a section of the planet and made more people and grew old and died. These people were sad when they died, because they had no place to go and even if they had someplace to go, they wanted to be where they had just been, because they missed the people and things they had left behind.

Infinity decided to take her little section of Space and make it a home to all these lost and lonely people. So every time a person died, a place was set for him in Infinity's section, where he could look down at the people and things he had left behind, disguised as a star.

And when the sun came out on the planet where he had been, and the stars were hidden for a while, the person got to play until night came and he could watch over his friends again.

And sometimes, when the person tried and when his loved one listened, they could have a conversation. Sometimes the conversation came in a dream, sometimes as a random thought, but it made the person very happy because he wasn't alone anymore, and the people he had left behind were not alone either.

Word got out among all the people of all the universes and soon Infinity's little section was nothing but a white sea of stars, so she called it The Milky Way.

Cabin in the Hollow

By Kat Martell

A TRUE STORY!

This is the true story of the camping trip I took with my father when I was ten years old. My dad was not the kind of guy to pull up to a nice spot in the KOA, near the johns. He was hardcore, and liked to find primitive spots, away from any sign of civilization. He carried in his own water, carried out his own waste. From his campsites, my dad would head off for hikes that lasted most of a day. He didn't tolerate a slacker. Complaints angered him. I learned to keep up, or find my way back to our tent alone.

My parents hadn't lived together since I was two, and I didn't know my father well. We had never spent much time together, other than on these summer camping trips. He wasn't much of a talker. We spent many hours, sprinkled throughout my childhood, hiking in silence. It was lonely, and it was also beautiful.

This particular summer, we went camping with his new wife, Karen. She rated a trip to a quaint cabin, complete with an outhouse and a river nearby. It was a five-mile hike down a steep, rocky grade in dense forest, carrying ten days' worth of food and gear, into a secluded valley in the Blue Ridge Mountains. He hadn't gone completely soft.

It was a long, hard hike down into the hollows. My dad had a map he'd received in the mail from the Shenandoah National Park office. It looked like a bunch of wavy concentric circles to me, not like any map I'd ever seen, but my dad said it would get us there as we walked. He told us stories about the mountain farmers who had lived in this area. They cleared their farmland out of the dense woods by hand, and a small community had grown here well over a hundred years ago. A man named John Corbin built the cabin we would be staying in. It was the only structure still standing; the only remains of a town which had died off slowly, as the people were forced out when the land became part of the National Park. My dad said that the Corbin family had held out longest, and was the last to go, in the early 1900s.

I noticed that he admired these people, for being tough and working hard to live and farm there. They had carved out a place for themselves in the world. My dad was talking more than I'd ever heard him talk, and I was glad. I was thankful that the hike was downhill, though after the first hour, my legs were burning, and finally went numb.

Reaching the bottom of the hollow late that afternoon, we found the clear, cold river we had been looking for. It was narrow here and could be crossed easily on foot. Soon, we came upon a clearing. There was a wide porch spanning the front of the cabin. The log building was small, one room with a fireplace and a rickety old table, behind it a small kitchen with a smaller cooking fireplace and wooden shelving along two walls. There was a staircase leading up to an attic bedroom. The cabin was dark, full of soot and dust. The sparse wooden furniture looked as though it had been there for a very long time.

I found a small building to the side of the main cabin, which was full of bunk beds, stacked three high, along each wall. There were no windows. It smelled musty and slightly sweet, and though it was a little bit spooky even in the light of day, I thought it would be cool to have my very own room. I set up my sleeping bag and ran off to help collect wood.

I could hardly keep my eyes open over dinner, which was cooked over a fire pit in the clearing. Karen lit a dim lantern, walked me to the outhouse, and then to my little bunk room. The light threw wild shadows across the walls and ceiling, and the smell seemed stronger now, almost putrid. Immediately, I felt unwelcome there. I forced my legs to carry me casually over to the bunk where my sleeping bag lay, and climbed in. Karen said good-night, and walked away with the lantern, closing the door behind her. I was in complete darkness. I listened to her footsteps fading, and heard her muffled conversation with my dad on the porch. They seemed very far away. I tried to get comfortable, wanting to be brave. Lying still, I listened hard into the black night.

I could hear faint creaking from the porch where my dad and Karen were moving around, the wind blowing the tall trees overhead. It was cold; I could not warm up enough to fall asleep. Just as my eyes were beginning to close, I heard a movement nearby, down at the foot of the bed. It sounded like a shuffling foot on the floor, or my backpack being pushed aside, sliding across the dusty wood.

I held my breath. I was too scared to call out, though even if I could have, I was just as scared to bother my dad. I wanted Karen to like me—I wanted to be tough. I lay awake for a long time in the still darkness. Though I didn't want to stay in that room, though I was tense, I was also very tired and soon fell asleep.

I woke some time later to the sound of another shuffle at the end of the bed. My eyes flew open, trying to see into the darkness. I heard the wind in the trees outside, but there were no longer any sounds of talking or movement from the porch.

Suddenly, I felt a finger tap-tap on my right arm, giving a little push. I whispered, "Daddy?" hoping against hope that he was the one standing beside me. No answer came. Screaming, "DADDY!!" I pushed out of my sleeping bag and bolted for the door. In the darkness I struggled with the door latch, panting and certain that something would grab me any second. With relief, I released the latch and threw the door open.

Running up the porch, I yelled for my dad over and over again. He met me at the bottom of the attic stairs, looking sleepy and annoyed. Throwing my arms around his waist, I told him that I could not sleep out there by myself. He asked why and I answered, "Too dark! Too smelly! Too scary!"

He got my sleeping bag for me, and I bedded down on the floor in front of the fireplace, relieved to have the light, and the grown-ups near by. I would have preferred to sleep upstairs with them, though my dad wouldn't hear of it. The dark doorway into the drafty little kitchen bothered me, as did the old front door that didn't latch well and rattled slightly in the breeze, but finally I drifted off.

***

I woke to the smell of bacon frying over the fire pit. All thoughts of spooky things were gone with the warm morning light. By day, the clearing around the cabin was beautiful. Birds sang, the tall grass waved in the gentle breezes, and the river mumbled its friendly song nearby.

I was excited to get exploring. The riverbed was rocky, and I walked a long way north, stepping stone to stone. Most of my days were spent up and down the river banks, building forts, making dolls out of sticks and bark, laying in the dappled sunlight telling myself stories. Twice, I felt like someone was watching me, and turned to look into the trees, but saw no one. Both times, I ran back to the cabin and stayed close for the rest of the day. I explained it to myself as a symptom of being alone in the woods—tricks of the sunlight filtering through the trees. In the evening, I brought water up from the river, helped with dinner and played games with Karen while my dad sat nearby.

On the fifth night I was in my sleeping bag on the floor, reading by firelight, when I heard the sound of footsteps just outside. They faded away as I put my book down. A few minutes later I heard the muffled voices of two women, but I could not make out their words. I thought they must be lost campers, though there was something eerie about it which held me still. Their voices seemed to fade in and out, mid-conversation, as though someone were turning up and down the volume on a radio. It grew quiet again, as I lay awake in the dying light from the fireplace.

The voices returned, louder this time. I was tired, tired of being frightened, and angry at those women for scaring me! Before I could think, I jumped up and strode over to the door, throwing it open. The voices instantly fell silent. The porch was empty. I slammed the door shut.

My dad called down, "Hey, what are you doing?"

I said, "Nothing! I heard something!"

He said, "We're in the woods! It's probably a raccoon! Go to bed!"

I got back into my sleeping bag. There was some comfort in knowing that if anything came in to get me, I could scream and my dad was right there. Eventually, I fell asleep, exhausted.

***

In the morning, when my dad went off in search of more firewood, I told Karen about the voices I had heard. She didn't believe me, but seemed amused, and said, "Well, I'll tell you what, I'll sleep down here with you tonight. I'd like to hear that for myself!"

That night, I felt safe and fell asleep easily. The fire had almost completely died out when I woke to the sound of the voices on the porch again. I nudged Karen who sat up like a shot, her eyes wide. She grabbed a poker from beside the fireplace, braced herself, and opened the door slowly, just a sliver, to peek outside. The voices stopped. She peered into the darkness, then closed the door gently. Sounding frightened, she whispered, "I wonder if I should wake your dad?" Just then, the voices started up again. Karen wedged a chair in front of the door, and we both went upstairs to sleep. I was allowed to sleep with them for the rest of the trip.

***

The days were active, busy with playing, hiking and helping with meals. I had grown tired of the river banks, and moved on to exploring the woods. On our last day there, I went farther from the cabin than I had before, and happened upon what seemed to be an overgrown path. Following it, I came to the stone foundation of an old building hidden in the underbrush, and searching the area, found four or five more. They were covered with plants and moss, hidden proof that there had once been a town in the hollow. I couldn't wait to tell my dad, knowing that he would be proud of me for exploring so far away on my own, and for finding the evidence of the town that he had not been able to find the whole time we were there.

On my way back to find the path, I noticed a rusted iron gate, covered with vines almost entirely hidden, standing just inches in front of a large tree that must have grown there since the gate was last used. I decided to see if there had been another building behind it, and found my way around, over a fallen log, pushing greenery aside. I soon noticed an odd rock at my feet. Kneeling down, I brushed away leaves and peeled off some moss. There was a name carved into the stone.

I was standing in the middle of a graveyard. The gravestones were so old that they had crumbled. They were mostly hidden by moss, with plants growing up through crevices in the stones and trees growing between them. I stood frozen for an instant, feeling as though there were a hundred eyes peering out at me from the woods all around. I clambered back over the fallen log and ran back through the woods to the cabin at a sprint.

***

Early the next morning we packed up our gear and were soon on our way up out of the valley. It was a long hike and hard going, but with every step I was closer to my dad's van with its radio that would play loud music all the way back to the city.

Every step brought me closer to my mom, who would pick me up the next day, and to finally going to bed safe and sound, curled in her arms.

Back home, anyone who asked me about the trip was told it was "Fine! Fun!" My nights at the cabin in the hollow made bedtime tough for a while, but their memory soon faded, like a scary movie that is eventually forgotten and lets you sleep with the lights out again.

***

Before that summer, I had never thought about ghosts. As time went on, it settled over me with certainty that some of the people who had built that little town in the hollow with their own hands, raised their children there, and died there, had never left.

Don't Read This Aloud!

By Oliver O'Rourke

Back in the 1800s, they say that a werewolf terrorized this part of the woods. A group of Russian settlers had traveled through the area looking for a new life in America and had passed though here on their journey. There were five people in the party of settlers, but one of the men had fallen ill and the settlers had to camp here for a few days until he was well enough to travel again. It is said that the man had been attacked by a silver wolf earlier on the journey and was nearly delirious from his gaping wound, a raw and wicked gash to his throat that had caused him much blood loss. He was pale and frail and so delirious that he could no longer speak.

A young woman in the party remembered tales of werewolves from the Russian countryside and was very wary of the situation. Day and night, she watched the injured man closely and brought him food and water. But he grew so weak that he could only lie in the back of the covered wagon, wrapped in his blood-soaked bandages.

Two nights later beneath a full moon, the young woman returned to the campsite after washing in the stream. She went over to check on the injured man, but found that he was missing from the wagon. Her heart was filled with sadness for she realized that he must have passed away while she'd been gone. She cursed herself for imagining that he might have been turning into a werewolf. As she made her way into the firelight to sit and mourn with the others, she discovered that the entire party had been massacred, the limbs ripped from their bodies by some terrible beast. In a panic, she called out for her father, but he too was missing.

Werewolf!

Heart thudding with terror, she quickly dug around in the wagon and found her father's box where he kept a silver knife. She struggled to remember the words of the spell she'd heard as a child when a werewolf had been discovered in her home village. Doing the best she could, she scratched down the words on a piece of leather and followed the hideous cry of the creature that echoed from deep within the woods. Although her mind was numb with fright, she followed the sounds for most of the night, knowing that she must find and destroy the creature—or become the next victim.

There on a moonlit ridge beneath a tall tree, she saw the gruesome shape of a half-man, half-beast, its misshapen body covered with spiky black hair, and fresh blood dripping from its trembling, snarling snout. Everything that had been human about the creature was now gone as its red eyes glared in the moonlight. As its powerful jaw snapped down on the arm it was gnawing, she recognized the ring on the hand's finger—her father's.

Silently, she prayed for strength to end the terror and avenge her father's death. Without thinking twice, the young woman crept up behind the hideous beast and plunged the silver knife deep into the thick, leathery skin of its back, piercing all the way through to its heart. With a blood-curdling howl, the creature slumped to the ground and returned to its human form.

Wasting no time, the girl dug a hole and buried the body in a shallow grave at the base of a nearby tree, reciting the old spell from the piece of leather. She prayed that the terrible creature would never rise again and ran away as fast as her legs would carry her. She knew that it would be safe to tell no one, for the fiend would stay dead as long as the spell to resurrect it remained buried with its bones. But if the words were to be repeated aloud, the spell would be broken and the werewolf would be free to rise from its grave and kill again.

Just last week, a story ran in the newspaper which backs up the facts you've been told. A local teenager was out hunting rabbits and had been at it all afternoon without any luck at all. Finally giving up, he headed home for dinner. As he made his way toward the cabin just on the other side of town, his dog began barking wildly at a hole at the base of a tree on the ridge. The teen poked around at the hole, hoping that there was a fat rabbit waiting within. But no rabbit emerged. The teenager continued prodding the ground with the butt of his gun, which eventually ran up against something hard. Digging around in the dirt, he unearthed a small wooden box. Not believing his good luck, he found a silver knife wrapped in a piece of leather with strange writing on it that he couldn't understand. But the gleaming old knife was a treasure that was sure to bring a good price at the local antique store.

The teenager took the knife straight into town where he sold it to the shopkeeper just before the store closed for the night, keeping only the piece of leather as a memento of his find. When the local paper got word of the story, a reporter went to the antique shop to take a photo of the knife, but found that it had been sold a day earlier to a tourist passing through town. No one knows what happened to the silver knife. But the writing on the piece of leather was translated from Russian into English and published in the local newspaper.

Hound of Hell!
Return to your demon master!
Be banished from this place
And never rise again,
Forever more, forever more!

Whatever you do, NEVER REPEAT these words aloud by the edge of the fire beneath the moonlight in the woods, or you risk your life and the lives of everyone in town!

The Old Man
By Barbara Bowman

It had been six days since Everett last saw anyone on the trail. He was following the two-thousand mile Appalachian Trail, which runs from Springer Mountain in Georgia north to Mount Katahdin in Maine. Each year thousands of people travel this trail, at least part of it, which passes along the ridgeline of the Appalachian Mountains.

Everett had become a bit disoriented when a small black bear had attacked his backpack for food, and Everett had fought him off. The bear had gotten away with the food, though, and Everett was left with a minor concussion. Without food, he was also becoming very weak and although he was skilled enough to capture and roast a few squirrels along the way, their bony, gamey bodies weren't enough to appease his rumbling gut.

Everett still had thirty-five miles to go to Erwin, Tennessee, a small village up in the Great Smoky Mountains where white folk have lived since the late 1500s. He was hoping he would see a fellow traveler who had food to share along the way, but no one was in sight. The trail was most popular in the summer, and now it was fall, with beautiful changing leaves but complete quiet desolation.

As dusk fell, Everett swept the forest with his eyes for any critters to calm his hunger when he spotted a light in the distance. With interest and hope, he quickly hobbled towards the beacon up ahead. As he neared his target he discovered that it was a small cabin, a bit run-down and shabby, but quaint and cozy, with lights aglow in the two small windows on either side of the door. In his excitement he climbed the stairs to the porch and knocked rapidly on the door. He heard shuffling, and the door creaked open. An old man stood before him, white skin and white hair almost matching, clothes ragged but warm. Everett explained his situation and the man happily asked Everett in.

"I don't see many folks around here," the old man said. "I keep to myself pretty much these days, but occasionally I get a wanderer off the trail."

The cabin only had one room, which was sparsely marked by a small bed and a rocking chair with a fireplace on one end and the two windows and door on the other. The man brought Everett a bowl of steaming stew from a kettle on the fire. Everett started gulping it down even though it burned his tongue. It was the best thing he had ever tasted. The vegetables must have been freshly dug and the meat was unlike any Everett had ever tasted before, like a cross between venison and rabbit, but even richer in flavor and complexity. Whatever it was, it was a welcome addition to his body. The warmth radiated from his stomach throughout his entire body to the frigid toes and appendages. He completed the first bowl quickly, and the man brought him more, smiling merrily and watching him eat. Within minutes, Everett downed three large bowls of the stew. His belly was distended and he felt like he would purr like a kitten if he could.

Everett's eyes became heavy, as he had been hiking all day. The man offered Everett the bed, saying that he himself slept in the chair, because it was more comfortable for him in his old age. He joked that he would never be able to get up if he lay down.

Everett crawled under the thick quilt, snuggled in tight, and looked at the fire one last time before he nodded off. He was so happy he had come across this cabin.

***

Everett opened his eyes. It was pitch black and smelled like dirt. He couldn't see anything, but he felt around. It was damp and cold. It was dirt. He heard the floors squeak above him, as the old man rocked in his chair, whistling a ditty of a tune fit for rocking on a front porch on a muggy summer evening. Everett thought he must be in the cellar. He had no idea how long he had been there. He felt around some more, and discovered the walls were lined with shelves of jars. Everett was confused as to the reality of what was going on. Where exactly was he, and how did he get there from that warm, cozy bed without waking up? As his hand slid over the jars, he caught one in his gangly fingers, causing it to crash to the ground with a loud thud. The rocking chair stopped squeaking. There was silence. Everett could then hear the old man shuffle across the floor, stopping directly above him. A door was opened, and Everett shielded his eyes from the light. It was day from the looks of it.

"You're a heavy sucker, young man," said the old man. "I bet you're the heaviest one yet. But that will be good for stew-makin'."

As Everett's eyes began to adjust, he looked around his cell and discovered what the jars were filled with. Eyeballs of varying colors filled one, while fingers of different sizes filled another. There were hundreds of them, filled with chunks of meat and body parts like ears, noses, and toes. Everett instantly knew what he had eaten, and his stomach began to churn from the very thought of it. But then he became mad, furious. He was boiling inside, and would never allow someone like this old deranged man to do this to him.

Everett leapt out of the cellar even though he was a good seven, eight feet down, surprising the old man, knocking him back against the wall. The old man then got angry, and came at Everett. They circled each other, arms outstretched, each ready to pounce at any moment. The old man hurled his gnarly and seemingly frail body at Everett, who was almost twice his size. Everett was amazed at the strength of the old man and really had to put all of his strength into keeping the old man back as he went for Everett's throat, getting closer and closer, seconds from gaining a strong, strangling grip. But Everett pulled strength from within himself that he wasn't even aware of before, and flung the old man to the ground. The old man pulled something from his pocket and held it in his hand.

"You see this?" the old man said, showing Everett a small shrunken head. "This is what happened to the last one who tried to escape." His deranged laugh bellowed throughout the cabin.

Not me, thought Everett, and he grabbed a log next to the fireplace, raised it above his head, and slammed it down with a bang. There was silence. Everett didn't look at what he had done. But he saw the old man's grip loosen on the shrunken head. Everett grabbed the shrunken head and stuck it in his pocket, almost like a reminder of what he had just escaped, and he ran out the door, backpack in tow. He looked back at the cabin just to make sure the old man wasn't after him. But he tripped and hit his head on a rock.

When he came to, Everett looked around. All he saw was his tattered backpack lying next to him. The cabin was nowhere in sight. Where could it be? Was this all a dream, a hallucination? Everett picked up his body and wiped himself off, when he felt something in his pocket. He reached in to find out what it was. Slowly, he pulled out the shrunken head.

The Cellar

By Tomi Lyn Bowling

As he peeked out from underneath the rickety old wooden steps in the cellar, the boy's heart raced so hard he was sure that the pounding noise would be heard by anyone else in the cellar. He trembled as he stood there peering out, looking for the source of the loud bang he had heard while upstairs. It was dark, cold and he was all alone in the five-story house on Kingswood Grove, in the tiny town of Douglas on the Isle of Man. The howling wind off of the Irish Sea pelted the house, shaking all of the windows and lifting a tile or two from the roof. It was not unusual for the electricity to be out in this kind of weather, and it was. Indeed, this was not the kind of night one would ever desire to be home alone.

He could smell the cold, damp air in the cellar as he cowered down and listened for any breathing or movement. He could see only the window on the far side of the cellar. The century-old building had a tiny window in the corner, but it was never cleaned, so the light was faint and it would be a challenge to make out any shapes outside. He had hoped the light from that window would help him to see. He tried to focus his eyes but could not see beyond this little cubby where the window was. He listened but did not hear anything. He grew more and more frightened as the whistling wind slipped through a tiny crevice in the window. Rain started to fall along with the wind, making it louder and harder to listen for any breathing or movement.

It was a stalemate. He knew he would have to make a move. He knew that the darkness held the patient but large figure of a man lurking in the cellar and just waiting to attack.

He closed his eyes and held his breath as he crawled out from beneath the stairs. He remained as quiet as possible. He could feel the air temperature suddenly drop but not enough to curtail the sweat that traversed his forehead. He stopped. He listened carefully. He heard movement. He felt something on his back as if there was someone breathing behind him. He knew, now, he was not alone. His terror grew as he stood out in the open, now vulnerable to his stalker.

His whole body trembled as he tried to remember the last time he saw the club his dad kept in the cellar. He remembered seeing it leaning against the wall beside him. He carefully slid his hand across the cold concrete, feeling his way to the club.

The rain started to pour down even harder. Now fearing he had made a mistake coming down here, he decided to look for a way out while still feeling the wall for the club. All that and more was racing through his mind, and then it dawned on him. He really wasn't alone. He had forgotten that upstairs on the third floor, his little sister lay sleeping. It was his job to look after her. His parents would be so unhappy if anything bad were to happen. He suddenly felt a little pinch of bravery return. He was still terrified but knew he had to get out of the cellar, and fast. He decided to make a run for it.

Bolting out like a bullet, he knocked over the club he had been looking for and charged up the stairs, feeling the presence of something trying to seize him on his way out. He could feel something grabbing for him. He slammed the cellar door shut and locked it. He ran to the kitchen to get one of his mother's kitchen knives. The lights came back on briefly. He took advantage of the light and ran up the stairs to check on his sister. She lay peacefully sleeping in her bed. As he went down the steps back to the living room the wind gave out a roar and the lights went off again.

He gripped the knife in his hand and guided his trip down the steps carefully holding on to the railing. As he approached the fifteenth stair (he always counted), he heard it again—BANG—a really loud bang coming from the cellar. His heart leapt and was pounding away again. He now worried that what he had thought was a sleeping sister was actually a dead one. Recalling the visit, he now realized she was perilously still. He wasn't sure. Was she dead or alive? He decided he was simply in a panic and she must've been sleeping, and he must protect her from the stranger lurking in the cellar.

He made his way back down the stairs to the main floor, walked over to the cellar door and slowly unlocked the door. He carefully and quietly opened the door and started his trip down the stairs. He could feel it again. There was something there. He spoke out in a quivering voice, "Who's there? I know you're in here. I've got a knife." These were some very big words for a boy not yet twelve years old.

No reply, only some movement: he could see motion to his left as if someone was hiding behind the workbench. He spoke out again, trying to appeal to the stranger. He eyed the stairs, contemplating running up them again. He feared this time he would not be so lucky as to get away. The motion started towards him and he could feel a cold breeze on his face. The boy was absolutely paralyzed from the fear now.

He could smell something that he could not put his finger on. It was an odd smell, a kind of stale smell, like opening an aged jar that had not been used in years. He tried to focus again to see if he could make out the figure of a man there. He could see only blackness, darkness, but it seemed thicker in the spot where he'd assumed the man was hiding.

He stepped backwards towards the bottom step, anticipating breaking free yet again. As he stepped back he lost his balance and fell. The knife flew out of his hand and out of view. He screamed out in terror as he felt the presence nearer to him. As he cried out, a loud noise upstairs sounded off, and he tried to stand.

At that exact minute the lights came back on, illuminating the cellar, and a voice called out, "Jeremy, what are you doing?" His father had returned home. When Jeremy looked at the spot where the presence had been, he was stunned to discover a cat had gotten in the cellar and was now staring back at him from the darkest corner, just as terrified as he had been. Right as Jeremy spotted the cat, his father noticed the knife and asked about it. Jeremy was most embarrassed at first but was soon relieved to discover his father was quite proud of him going down to the cellar to protect his sister.

The Bear Story
By Rebecca Mate

Pine trees stretched towards sunshine from the interlaced pine-needle floor of the forest. We were at a fork in the trail; serious campers went right, day hikers went left. My brother, Andy, stood in front of a weathered wooden sign taller than he was, staring at the picture of a menacing bear with glinting teeth.

"Mom," said my wimpy, eight-year-old brother, "Why does it say what to do when you see a bear?"

Being the older brother by four years, I knew the answer to that one. I turned around and raised my arms above Andy. My dad had given me a warm furry brown coat last month, with a hood, so I tried to be as bear-like as possible when I loomed over him and said, "Because a bear has big teeth and HE'LL EAT YOU!! GRRRRRR!"

"David!" snapped my mother.

"GRRRRR!" I repeated and gave my little brother a not-so-gentle bear hug. He screamed like a girl.

"David Leonard Brown!" my mother said, apparently calling upon the strength of my great, great grandfather, Trapper Leonard.

I let go and she, clumsy with a huge backpack, knelt down next to Andy and pointed to the sign. She said, "That's good, dear. See, it says here that if you make noise by yelling or clapping, wild animals will stay away."

Andy read from the list, "1. Never run from a bear, 2. Never turn your back on a bear, 3. Never feed a bear, 4. Never chase or pet a bear." He looked at the picture of the bear on hind feet, mouth opened in a roar and said, "Pet a bear?!"

My dad looked over his shoulder and read, "Bear sign: small cow-patty shaped pile of poop. Content is mixed berries, birdseed, and coils of plastic bags. Moss and vegetation torn up and scattered. Rocks turned over for grubs and roots..."

Mom sat down on a rock, bringing out the comfort of a slice of white bread with peanut butter. I slipped off my pack and rolled sleeping bag, and scaled the rock face behind her.

"Are we going to run into a bear?" asked Andy.

"Not likely," said Dad, slipping off his pack for a chance to rest near Mom. He had to carry the tents.

"I knew I should have brought the honey sticks," said Mom, struggling with a spoon and honey jar, getting her hands all sticky with nowhere to wash them off.

Andy pawed around in her food pack and pulled out a can of evaporated milk, "Cool! Can I have this?"

"No, Andy," she said, "We need it for cereal tomorrow morning. I've got every meal planned out exactly. David, do you want a peanut butter sand... David?"

"Up here, Mom," I said, from a narrow ledge three stories high.

"David," said Dad, "Come on down from there!"

"Not a bear in sight," I said, looking around.

"Must we mention bears?" asked my mother, glancing over at Andy.

"Maybe, since our last name is Brown, we're related," said my Dad, reading the bottom of the sign, "After all, the word 'bear' comes from an Old English word that means 'brown animal.'"

Mom laughed. Then she heard the rocks skitter, saw me and panicked when my left foot slipped a few inches on the descent. "What are you thinking?"

"Don't worry, Mom," I said, "years of climbing fake rocks at the mall has prepared me for this moment."

Once down, I dashed up the trail.

"Your sandwich?" she asked, sticky hand outstretched.

"I saw a deer from up there, with a white tail," I called out, my fuzzy brown hood bobbing behind me as I ran. Wildlife seemed more important than food at that moment.

A chipmunk scurried away from whatever danger I appeared to be running away from. An all-white butterfly flitted from wildflower to wildflower in the clearing where the deer had been.

I walked back. "No jelly?"

"We voted, remember?"

"Oh, yeah." I took the sandwich and leaned up against a pine. For some reason, food always tasted better in the fresh-air mountains after a long hike.

When I loaded up my brother with his pack so we could take the right fork of the trail, I noticed that he had a lump in his shirt about the size of a can of evaporated milk, but I didn't say anything.

***

That night at the campsite I had to sleep in a tent with my brother. I couldn't stand up in the tent and with two sleeping bags rolled out there was only an eight-inch walkway between.

The ground seemed lumpy at first, but I knew we were both so tired it wouldn't matter.

"Will a bear be able to rip a hole in our tent?" asked Andy.

"Know why they call them teddy bears?" I asked him.

"No," he said, settling into his sleeping bag as if for story time.

"Over a hundred years ago, the President of the United States, President Theodore Roosevelt, went on a bear hunt in Mississippi. They couldn't find a bear for three days, but finally found one. He didn't want to shoot it because it was old and hurt, so he asked someone else to put it out of its misery. A newspaper guy that draws cartoons made one to show how President Roosevelt refused to shoot the bear. This store owner guy named Morris got the President's okay to call two bears his wife made 'Teddy's bears.' He put them in his store's window. And a German woman sewed stuffed animals like elephants and bears, and Americans bought them starting in 1903. Some of her bears were used as table decorations when Theodore Roosevelt's daughter got married, so people started calling them teddy bears. At least, that's what my teacher told me."

It had worked. He was asleep. I soon followed.

Some flapping noise woke me up in the middle of the night. The tent flap fluttered against the tent letting in a little moonlight. Andy wasn't in his sleeping bag.

I called for him quietly.

"He's with us," Mom reassured me from her tent next to ours.

I really needed to do something to toughen up that kid so he wouldn't grow up and be a scaredy cat.

I went back to sleep, but stirred a little when Andy came back in later. I heard him poke a hole in the evaporated milk, probably how Dad taught us to do it with a quick hit on the knife handle, to drive the point into the can. He drank it rather noisily, but that didn't stop me from drifting off to sleep.

***

The next day was colder. As we all sat around with individual packages of dry cereal, Andy tried to deny that he drank the milk last night. Fortunately Mom had three more cans.

"Just admit it. Get in trouble and get it over with," I told him, out of earshot of our parents.

"Yeah, why don't you?" he countered.

"I don't even like the stuff," I said. I pulled my furry coat around me, wishing I had a warm breakfast like bacon and eggs, or even oatmeal.

It warmed up for a few hours in the middle of the day when we were exploring the woods around our campsite. We found some bear poop, and called Dad over, but he said it was at least a week old, judging by what he had read on the sign about how to tell.

"At least it's not steaming," he joked.

There was a nice rock face at the edge of our campsite. I was eyeing it as I came to see what Mom had for dinner. "Don't even think about it," she said.

***

Come evening, my coat and I were huddled as close to the campfire as possible without getting singed. Five marshmallows later, I was able to back off a bit.

Once we were in the tent for the night, I was debating whether to leave my coat on inside the sleeping bag. Mom had warned against it, saying I'd get too hot. I flipped open the bag and was lying there in my coat, trying to decide, when I fell asleep.

What seemed like many hours later, I became aware that Andy had curled up next to me.

"Get in your own bag!" I said.

"I am," he said sleepily.

On some level, I realized I should have noted that his voice seemed too far away, but I was tired of him wimping out all the time. I turned over and gave him a little shove, and said, "I mean it!"

There was a grumble.

My eyes flew open and tried to adjust to the dim light in the tent.

My hand hadn't met the cloth of the long-sleeved knit shirt over the little shoulder of my brother. No, I had just shoved something furry.

Had he pulled part of my coat over him?

As I became more and more awake, I knew for sure that the fur on that shoulder was much different than my coat.

"Andy, open the tent flap," I said.

"Why?" he asked.

"I want to show you my teddy bear," I said, trying to be calm.

"What?" he asked, but he pushed open the flap. The moonlight reached in and showed us the bear cub that was snuggling up next to me.

The cub wasn't too happy about this disturbance to his sleep. He got up on all fours and shook, giving a louder grumble. Even a small bear has large teeth.

Andy could have been a statue, arm holding open the tent flap, mouth agape.

"Go get Dad," I said. My little brother could no more move from that spot than if I had glued his feet to the tent floor.

I waved my arm, gesturing Andy to get out while he could.

The bear cub took this to mean, "Let's play," and he nuzzled at my furry coat with his nose. He wrestled me over. He was even stronger than Dad.

"He thinks you're his brother," said Andy.

I didn't want Mom waking up in the morning to an empty tent that used to house her two sons. I didn't care what the sign said; I ran out of there, grabbing Andy like a football on the way out. I shoved him in the direction of our parents' tent.

The moon was bright, illuminating the forest in its spooky reflected-light sort of way.

The bear cub poked his head out of the tent, as if looking to see where his playmate had gone. I growled at the bear to give Andy a chance to run.

I ran for the nearest tree with low branches and climbed as if my life depended on it. About twelve feet up, I had reached the limb where Dad had hung the food for the night.

I looked down.

The little bear was right behind me. He nuzzled up against my leg.

I went out on a limb, literally.

"David!" exclaimed my mother, as she followed Dad out of their tent.

"He's the one who drank the milk!" said my brother, pointing at the bear, like a lawyer defending his client.

"I'll get him some more," I said, reaching down off the limb into the food bag. The milk wasn't readily available at the top of the backpack.

The little guy batted a paw at my coat. Could this limb hold the both of us?

As cold as it was, I slithered out of my coat and shook it at the cub, then dropped it. He looked from me to the coat, back and forth a couple of times, trying to wrap his bear wits around "taking off one's coat." Then he climbed down the tree to wrestle with this furry outer covering.

I reached deeper into the bag and grabbed something round and hard.

At that moment, I heard the loudest noise I think I have ever heard come from the mouth of a wild animal. It was a roar to strike fear into the hearts of even the bravest of men.

We all looked past the tents to see what had to be Mother Bear, and we peered down into her foghorn mouth past all those sharp teeth.

Dad, Mom and Andy froze together like a single statue in the park, facing the mother bear. Andy tried to follow the directions on the sign and make noise, but it just came out as a squeak.

Mother Bear, brown and fast, lumbered over to smell the furry coat her cub was practically wearing. She stood up on her hind feet and roared at me, so close I could almost smell her breath.

I lost my grip on the branch, and slid off, but managed to grab the food backpack. It couldn't hold me. We dropped to the ground at the bear's feet.

A can of milk rolled out of the pack and the cub pounced on it. He poked it with a claw and the white milk surfaced. His mother cuffed it away from him, sniffed at it, licked it and then pushed it towards him, as if approving of his find. He held it with both paws, like a baby on its back with a bottle, and enjoyed himself immensely drinking every sweet drop of it.

Mother Bear turned back to deal with me.

Dad shoved Mom and Andy into the tent, grabbed a radio and turned it up full blast. Click. No reception.

I was sitting on the cold ground, arms behind me holding me up, leaning back. Mother Bear came closer, sniffing at me.

Dad began yelling and waving his arms. Mother Bear glanced over at him, then turned back. Sniffing. Sniffing.

Suddenly, I realized that I still had the hard, round object in my hand, and I knew what it was, because it was a little bit sticky—the honey for the peanut butter sandwiches.

It was time to break another of the rules on the sign. I slowly brought my hand around, unscrewed the lid, set it down and backed away, head bowed, as if giving an offering to a god.

This jar of honey was of definite interest to the bear. Even the cub, now full of evaporated milk, came to investigate. His mother, at first, wouldn't let him have any, then relented, letting him get the final bits of honey in the jar.

***

While they feasted on their favorite treat, all of us humans were climbing that moonlit rock face. Even Andy, who was too scared to climb the fake rock at the mall, even with ropes, climbed with us. In fact, he was the first to reach the top.

The larger bear looked up at us once, just before scattering the contents of our food bag, but seemed disinterested.

Our family sat at the top of the rock, feet hanging down. My dad held me inside his coat for warmth, and Mom held onto Andy for comfort.

After a while, the mother and cub lumbered away together, but not before the cub swatted and wrestled with my coat a few more times.

***

We stayed up on that rock for a good hour after they left. And none of us got any sleep the rest of the night.

I continued to wear the coat, despite a few claw holes here and there, until everyone back at school knew the bear story.

Eva's Phone Call

By Susan Stroh

A TRUE STORY!

My son Chris listened to the voicemail and said, "Mom, there's this phone message for you but it's in a weird language."

He handed me the receiver. The voice was Eva's, calling from Finland. Her voice was clear, strong and urgent.

She's the only person in the world who says my name that way—"Sooizie," I thought, smiling. *But how odd that she spoke the rest of her message in Finnish; she knows I've forgotten my Finnish!*

Memories of Finland were always anchored to the first time I met Eva. I was sixteen, waiting in the railway station in Helsinki to meet the family I'd be staying with as an exchange student. Some of the Finnish families had claimed their American students and I became increasingly anxious watching my friends whisked away by their new families.

Eva and her family came out of nowhere, holding a picture of me out in front of them. Eva was young and sparkly-eyed and when she recognized me she laughed, opening her arms wide.

"Sooizie, I'm Eva, your Finnish mother!"

"You're so beautiful!" was all I could find to say to her.

"And you are our lovely American girl, we greet you with our hearts."

I had studied the language so diligently back then, but in 30 years had had no use for it, really. I'd seen Eva and my Finnish family three times since that time, but not for the past dozen years. Her voice always warmed me.

I immediately called Irina in Hollywood, a movie star from Finland, and asked her to translate the message.

She wasn't in.

By now, my husband Duane had come in from his pottery studio, his curiosity roused by our excitement. He agreed that Eva's message required immediate action, that I should call her right away.

"Maybe Kaija is sick or something," he said.

Kaija was my same-aged Finnish sister. During our year together, she and I shared everything from insecurities to dreams, frailties to fantasies. Heide was the younger sister and my Finnish brother Ilkka was the middle child.

I called Eva's flat in Helsinki. Heide answered the phone from a deep sleep. I asked for Eva, saying that she had called me several hours ago, but that I had just received the message.

"Oh Susie, Eva couldn't have called you, she's in the hospital with a terrible cancer. She hasn't spoken for days."

I was stunned. What my ears and heart had told me was now completely nullified. "I didn't even know she was sick, Heide. I'm terribly sorry."

"I'm sorry we didn't call you, Susie, but it was so sudden. They discovered stomach cancer a few weeks ago and Eva just gave in. I've been up with her for two days. Could we speak tomorrow? I can't even think straight."

I agreed we'd talk the next day.

Hearing my anguish, Duane held me and told me he'd send me back right away to see Eva. I wanted to see her, desperately. But how? On two artists' salaries, I hadn't been able to go back to see my Finnish family in twelve years, and only then because I'd directed a marketing video for Finnair.

A few minutes later, Irina called me back and listened to the message.

"Okay, here's what she said to you: 'Susie, come celebrate with us all night long and please bring some food.'"

I was perplexed. I told Irina what Heide had said about Eva's inability to speak. Irina sighed, "Let me hear the message again." I replayed it several times.

"Susie, I believe Eva contacted you. Reading between the lines, I'm convinced she really wants to see you."

Excited by Irina's confirmation of my gut feelings, I told Chris and Duane. "Eva means for me to come and celebrate Midsummer Night with them; it's the best all-night celebration I know. Remember, Duane, how awesome the bonfire was, built over the sea? And daylight all night? And the singing and dancing? And the feasting!"

"Was I there?" asked Chris.

"You were, but you were only two."

"But honey," Duane interjected, "it's a month away and she sounds so ill."

"I know," I said, deflated again.

"Mom, you know what I think? I think if you go back for Midsummer Night, she might get well."

"Oh, Chris, that would be so good. I taught Eva the swing dance years ago and we did that at Midsummer Night together. Remember, Duane?"

"Oh yeah, you and Eva were amazing!"

"When I spoke with her at Christmas she said it had been too long not seeing her daughter. She said she felt old. I had reassured her that we would plan a trip soon," I said sadly.

"We'll make it happen, honey."

The whole next morning I was on fire with the idea of going back. I rummaged through our savings account passbooks, my old money-hiding places, and figured out what I could sell. I thought that maybe I could up my fees on the newsletters I was designing. Maybe Duane could double the prices at his ceramic sale.

Over and over I asked myself, *what did she mean by "Please bring some food"?*

As an exchange student I had brought gifts of cake mixes and packaged puddings and Eva had laughed at the novelty of them. Was that it? Did she want me to bring something uniquely American again?

At noon I heard from Kaija. "Susie, Eva died in the night, at one a.m. our time."

"Oh, Kaija, I'm so, so sorry." There was a silence in which we both heard our voices catch on tears.

Finally Kaija continued, "Oh, Susie, we are all so amazed at the timing of your phone call to Heide. It was two hours after she died. We Finns believe that the spirit leaves the body two hours after death. Of course, Heide didn't know Eva had died when you called her. Ilkka stayed at the hospital to let us get some sleep. He just called with the news this morning.

"Oh, Kaija."

"Heide said you thought you received a phone call from Eva yesterday?"

I figured out the time difference and told her, "Eva called at 12:58 this morning your time, it's on my voicemail. I saved the message in case you ever want to hear it."

"That was two minutes before she died… It's impossible, of course, she couldn't speak at all…"

Silence.

"Someday, I'd like to hear it, but not now."

More silence.

"Susie, I just don't know what to think. If you did have some contact from Eva, even if I don't understand how, it does give me hope. It gives us all hope, somehow. And you know Ilkka, how skeptical he is, but he said, 'Eva would contact Susie, because Susie is so open to that kind of thing.'"

I brimmed up with tears again. Then I mustered the strength to ask, "When will you have the funeral?"

"Eva wanted it the day after Midsummer's Eve," Kaija said.

"I'll be there, if you want me to come."

Kaija gave in to her tears. "I would cherish your presence, but I can't ask you to make that sacrifice. Besides, it won't be such a jolly time as most Midsummer Nights."

I knew how close Eva and Kaija were. I knew how difficult it would be now for Kaija—for everyone.

Eva was there whenever I needed arms to hold me, always encouraging, always a light touch to serious subjects. Her laughter could dissolve pain. Eva was a friend, who for no reason I could discover, just decided to love me.

"I'll be there," I said to Kaija.

Midsummer Night was rainy, but we feasted in-doors around Eva's table. The children performed dances while the adults enjoyed the finest dilled salmon and aged wines. Late into the evening we sang all the old songs. But we didn't celebrate all night, not this time. Soon after midnight, we embraced each other and murmured soft words of comfort and love to each other before we all went off to our beds.

The day of the funeral I sat next to Ilkka, who had recently married a much younger woman. Their baby, Putte, was just two weeks old.

During the funeral Putte cried only once. Instinctively, I reached for him and rocked him. In my arms, he instantly stopped crying.

At the reception, when he was blissfully falling to sleep in my arms after a nice warm bottle of goat's milk, I finally figured out what Eva had meant by saying, "Please bring some food."

"You're hungry in your new body, aren't you, my friend?" I whispered over the concerto music that was playing.

He grinned and his eyes got sparkly. "Thank you for coming," the baby seemed to say, as blink-lessly, he looked straight into my soul.

"I love you, dear one," I said as I pulled him up onto my shoulder. His breath was sweet on my neck as we slowly, gently danced together once more.

A Crack in the Lake

By Kay Farkas

It was one of those regular summer afternoons; kids impatiently lined up beside the lake for their ride on the giant, yellow banana boat, better known to Alex and Tom as "Big Yeller."

"We'll never get our turn, you know that!" said Tom as he kicked a rock into the water.

"Whatever," Alex moaned. "It'll be dark soon, anyway."

Later that evening the wind curled dust and sand around the cabin, trees creaked and small whitecaps foamed across the lake. A faint aroma of hotdogs and onions wafted through the air.

Tom and Alex took their hotdogs down to the lake's edge, found a comfy spot and ate in silence.

"I don't want you guys wandering off, okay?" Tom's mother shouted from the cabin porch.

Tom waved back.

"Bummer we didn't get to ride Big Yeller," Alex said with a mouthful.

Tom nodded.

With full bellies the two gazed at the moon's glow upon the water. It suddenly dawned on them that it was quiet. Tom let out a "*Whoop, whoop!*" then hysterically laughed as he listened to his echo.

"Whoop! Whoop!"

As if an unseen force hit a switch, the lake stilled. Black clouds grew over the mountains beyond the lake. The boys looked at each other and frowned.

Across the lake…

CRACK.

"Did ya hear that?" Tom choked, as he spat a half-eaten hotdog bun into the air.

"Shhhh," Alex put his finger up to his lips.

CRACK!

CRACK!

"HELLO!" Tom yelled into night.

"Shhhh!" spat Alex.

They ran back to the cabin, grabbed their flashlights and went straight into their mom's room. The bed was empty. They ran through each room… nobody. They called out… nothing. They ran outside, called again… nothing. They tore up the path to a neighboring cabin, frantically knocked on the door… nobody. They ran into the general store, called out, but… nobody. Tom shone his light upon a phone hanging on the wall next to a barrel-sized jar of pickles, picked up the receiver and listened for the dial tone—dead. He banged the receiver on the counter several times, hung up then tried again—the phone made a faint "crack, crack" in his ear. He suddenly dropped the receiver, turned to Alex and stared; tears stung his eyes.

"Nobody's here, they're all gone!" Alex said as he threw himself against the counter.

Tom grabbed Alex by the arm and the two frantically ran back through the trees. Alex puffed, "It's a dream, it's just a bad dream."

Back in the cabin they sat and watched the moon's reflection on the lake, waiting for the…

CRACK…

CRACK!

Tom froze, Alex jumped.

CRACK!

"We're dead meat, Alex!"

The sky lit up and then…

CRAAAACK! came from outside the cabin door.

"Go on, open the door, Tom," Alex whispered.

"Are you kidding me? You do it!"

Alex slowly opened the door; both boys stepped outside onto the front porch.

"Hey, Tom, look at this!" Alex shouted.

Tom shone his light onto the front door, winced and held his nose as a strange slime oozed its way across the doorway.

CRACK!

CRACK!

Tom and Alex screamed, ran inside and slammed the door.

CRACK!

"STOP IT! Go away!" Tom cried.

"Too late," a voice gurgled from within the cabin.

"Go away!" Tom pleaded.

"Too late," the voice gurgled through the blackness.

By this time the green ooze had slimed its way under the cabin door, making its way across the floor.

"What do you want?" Tom screamed at the top of his lungs.

"What is mine," the voice whispered, gurgled, then spat in Tom's ear. Slime globbed onto his shirt, slithered down his pant leg and fell onto the floor.

"Give you what?" Tom cried.

"Give it to me and I'll give you yours." A foul stench filled Tom's nostrils as he collapsed, unable to breathe. Something lifted him into the air; his body slowly contorted, wrung one way, then the other.

"Leave him alone!" Alex screamed.

Tom dropped to ground, wheezing and coughing.

"Give me what's mine, I'll give you yours," the voice trailed off over the cabin and across the lake.

"What—what does this thing want?" Alex shouted as he threw himself on the ground beside Tom.

"We're gonna die," Tom moaned as he sat frozen to the ground.

Moments passed, then both agreed to find this "thing" whatever it was and give it back. They both grabbed flashlights and tore the cabin apart, looking for anything they could imagine giving to this unseen voice to make it go away: food of all sorts, toilet paper, toothpaste, knives, forks, clean and dirty linens, all of which they took and chucked into the lake.

Across the lake...

CRACK!

Shoes, socks, pants, chairs, into the lake.

CRACK!

CRACK!

"Let's face it, it's no use," Tom panted.

They hurried along the edge of the lake, their flashlights shining up and down rocks, through trees and bushes, into gullies. They both looked and tossed anything they could find into the lake.

Tom's flashlight shone through the pitch-blackness and into Alex's eyes. "What if we're the last two on earth?"

Alex said nothing, turned and walked ahead through dense trees and bushes, into the silent dark. Tom caught up.

They walked for hours, calling into the night in hopes of finding another living person. No echo, not a sound. They both collapsed on the ground. The faint glow of their flashlights finally died.

"Hello! Hello! Is anyone there?" a voice called through the night.

Alex lifted his head and strained to hear.

"Over here!" Alex cried.

The voice came closer. It was Ol' Man Tate.

The old man asked, "What are you two doing out here in the middle of the night?"

On their way to the old man's cabin, they told of what had happened and finished up their story, drinking lemonade on his porch. The old man hung his head and listened, patiently waiting for them to finish. Then he began to tell his tale.

Over fifty years ago, Tate and his partner, Gribble, made a deal—call it a deal of a lifetime: a fifty-fifty split on the gold found in and around the lake. They worked day and night, dredged and panned, filling sack after sack of the purest gold, which they hid on the other side of the lake. There the gold would stack, hidden in a secret cave.

It wasn't long after that Gribble went crazy. One night it got bad.

Tate caught Gribble wielding a hunter's knife. Gribble threatened to gut Tate and slice him piece by stinking piece. Gribble wanted all the gold and said Tate should leave and never return, if he knew what was best.

Tate couldn't take any more. He shot Gribble in the back; and after making sure he was good and dead, stuffed the body into a sack, heaved it into a boat and motored to the other side of the lake. There he made sure the sack was good and heavy and pushed Gribble over the side. Gribble sank fast. Tate stayed near to make sure the body wouldn't float to the surface. Then he left, moored the boat, and up he went to get his gold.

He took enough of the gold to build the lake's cabins, general store, an access road and the like. The rest he buried under a cabin. He had the resort ready, but for one reason or another something prevented it from being opened, until this year.

Tate finished his story and looked at the boys, searching for any pity they may have felt.

"Which cabin did you bury the gold under?" Tom asked Tate.

Tate hesitated then said, "Yours. I buried the gold under your cabin."

Tom and Alex stood up and both wanted to hit Tate square in the face. Together they both knew what this "thing" wanted… *gold*!

"You have to come with us, now!" Tom grabbed Tate's arm.

The three stumbled back through the woods towards the boys' cabin.

CRACK!

The noise made Tate jump but he didn't say a word.

"Don't tell me you can't hear that!" Tom yelled at Tate.

"Faster, ol' man!" Alex hissed.

They reached the cabin. All three leaned against the cabin's rail and caught their breath.

"Where is it?" Tom screamed to Tate.

Tate pointed towards the cabin door. The three ran inside.

CRACK!

Tate hobbled to the back of the cabin, squatted and lifted a trapdoor; then he disappeared into the hole as the boys stood near the edge and peered into the black.

Bag upon bag of gold was hauled up through the trapdoor.

CRACK!

CRACK!

"Hurry!" Alex screamed down the hole.

Finally Tate and the last bag came through.

CRACK!

A stench filled the cabin; slime oozed up through the floorboards and around the trapdoor.

"Now I'll take what's mine," the thick voice whispered.

Globs of slime licked, then swallowed bag after bag of precious gold.

This was the end. It got what it wanted. The ooze curled and sucked its way through the floorboards with a pop.

The three stood in silence, gazing at the floor.

Alex and Tom stared at the old man as he clutched his chest and slumped to the floor. Droplets of black water made puddles as the old man was slowly devoured. The boys backed away and watched in horror as piece by stinking piece the old man slid through a crack in the floor.

"A deal's a deal," gurgled in Tom's ear.

The rotten smell and ooze had gone.

"It's over," Alex said as he hugged his brother.

They both left the cabin and headed slowly to the water's edge, sitting where they had eaten the night before.

The wind blew softly through the trees and white caps danced upon the lake.

"You boys better come in now, looks like a storm's heading this way," yelled Mom from the front porch of the cabin. "And bring your plates with you, please."

Both boys picked up their plates and ran as fast as they could back to the cabin, hugging their mom as they laughed and cried.

"What's with you two?" Mom smiled.

The boys looked up and grinned.

"Now, clean yourselves up, we've got a visitor," Mom said.

The boys washed up, put on clean clothes then joined Mom on the porch.

"Tom, Alex, I'd like you to meet Mr. Gribble. He's taking over Mr. Tate's job."

"Lovely to see you, boys," sneered Mr. Gribble as he shook Tom's hand.

The Truth Be Told

By Barbara Bowman

Ryan, a burly man of twenty-seven, along with three of his friends, raced a crowded Jeep down a dirt road, leaving a trail of dust in their wake. Ryan needed to do some research in order to finish his Masters in Cultural Anthropology and so was leading his group on an excursion to explore a local legend. It had remained a deep mystery, even after all these years.

In 1874, a group of thirty-nine white ex-convicts made their way from Boston to the Black Hills of South Dakota. Led by John McCready, they were in pursuit of wealth during the gold boom of that time. Historians wrote that the group settled in a dense forest near Inyan Kara, a sacred mountain to the native Lakota people. Reportedly, McCready and his group of degenerates built log cabins, wrote to others back East about their gold successes and even sent pictures, but then they suddenly disappeared and were never heard from again. What was stranger still was that there was no sign left that they had even been there. No spaces with cut-down trees, no domesticated animals, and strangest of all, no log cabins. Many theories had been postulated, such as that they never were there in the first place, but had escaped to some other area of the Wild West in order to throw everyone off back East. But no one had been able to propose *where* that somewhere else would have been. Most history books speculated that the men were savagely killed by the Lakota, even though this was a weak theory, as there was no proof whatsoever of this occurring.

***

With Ryan were his girlfriend Adrianne and his buddies Craig and Steve, who were all there to help with the research.

Ryan was skeptical that the group of ex-convicts had ever really been there, and he planned to prove his theory in his thesis. He needed to be there, in that space, to gather the facts to support this hypothesis. But even with his skepticism, there was a nagging question in the back of Ryan's mind about the area where they had reportedly settled, because some people claimed that an unusually large number of people would go hiking in the forest but never return. In fact, this forest had the highest disappearance rate in the country. Ryan thought it was probably due to the area's high population of mountain lions and bears, but strangely, there were never any signs that the missing people had ever even been there. There was just the forest.

***

Ryan and his group arrived at the site. It was beautiful. The trees were thick with leaves, the plants were juicy and healthy, and the air was sweet. It was perfect, and so inviting. Ryan and the gang set out on foot with their backpacks and a GPS.

When they arrived at the spot where the thirty-nine settlers had reportedly built their homes, the trees were dense, meaning no homes could have been built there. But Ryan then looked at a satellite-view photograph of the forest, which showed a clearing exactly where they were standing—within a hundred yards of Inyan Kara. He looked up from the photograph and sure enough, there was Inyan Kara exactly where it was supposed to be. But how could this be? Perhaps they had found the wrong area, he thought, because the trees in this spot were hundreds of years old, and couldn't have grown since the settlers were supposedly there. But the GPS corresponded with the satellite image. He suggested they walk around this area, since perhaps they were just slightly off from the spot they were looking for. They split up and walked out in different directions.

Craig, an awkwardly tall and gangly man in his late twenties, with a long, scruffy beard, started heading west. He saw something dark on the ground in the distance. It didn't fit into the surroundings, so he approached it. As he neared the object, he saw that it was a small stone well. He was amazed because it looked like it was recently built, as there was no moss growing on the stones and the structure was not crumbling. He decided to look inside, but as he leaned over, a force swept him down into the well, which then disappeared, leaving a patch of green grass.

Adrianna, who was in her early twenties and fresh-faced, looked up and down the forest as she walked, searching for any piece of evidence. Just then, a beautiful deer went bounding by, so close that Adrianna could feel a cool breeze against her skin. She watched it. It stopped and turned back, looking at her. The deer motioned to Adrianna with its head for her to look at a particular tree. Adrianna's eyes traveled curiously over the tree. It must have been the largest tree in the forest, as it was standing a good twenty feet above the canopy and had twice the girth as the others surrounding it. The deer then turned and continued through the trees, almost disappearing in the mist. Adrianna approached the behemoth tree. She glided her hand over its surprisingly smooth bark. There were ridges, but the texture was as smooth as silk. Adrianna was mesmerized with how unusual this tree was. Suddenly and with no warning, it engulfed her by opening up its large trunk and wrapping itself around her, consuming her completely, leaving no sign that she was ever there.

Steve, Ryan's best friend and fellow Master's student, stomped through the brush. Nothing was standing out to him, and he kept drudging on even as the sun was fading. Just then, a small black beetle crawled up his sleeve, going unnoticed. Steve continued on, grumpy in the cold dampness of the forest, his stomach empty and growling. The beetle lightly climbed up his neck. Without his noticing, the beetle dug into his skin and crawled into his body. Shortly thereafter, Steve became woozy and started stumbling around. The forest was spinning and pulling in all directions, his arms loose and his body heavy. He tried to scream, but he could not. He tried and tried, panic rising as he found that he was voiceless. He tried to take a step, but it was as if his body was weighed down with sacks of sand. Millions of insects began to march up his clothing, soon covering him entirely. He was writhing in pain, but was unable to scream or move. Hordes of snakes ascended his body and slithered ferociously. He was covered entirely by the insects and snakes. No longer could his face be seen—only the form of what was once a man. The motion of the insects and snakes could be heard, like an eerie rustling of leaves. The insects and snakes quickly consumed him and the form that once was his body descended to the ground. Steve was gone, eaten completely. As easily as they arrived, the insects and snakes left, and silence filled the space.

***

Dusk was heavy now, and Ryan was beginning to become concerned that he could not find his friends. He called out to them, his voice echoing throughout the empty forest. He heard no return call. He looked at his GPS and then looked at the satellite photograph where the clearing was shown. Then he saw something move on the photograph. Thinking it was a bug, he shook the paper, but upon closer examination, he saw that it was him! He was in the photograph. He also saw his friends, looking like black dots on the ground from a plane. They all looked up at him from the photograph, and one by one they disappeared. Ryan was so scared that he dropped the photograph and started running. He ran and ran, but then he came upon a clearing. He looked at his GPS and saw that he was in the same location from where they had begun their search, with Inyan Kara also exactly where it was before. But there had been no clearing here before. How could this be? He ran again in what he thought was a straight line, but he returned to that very spot. The GPS indicated he was still there. His entire body was tingling in fear and his heart was beating so hard he felt his eyeballs pulsating with each beat. The forest suddenly went quiet.

Teepees appeared before his eyes. A small group of Lakota Indians went about their business, not noticing Ryan as he stood there watching in awe. The women were making dinner over fires; children were running around, playing. The men were relaxing, talking and laughing, joking around with each other. A scream rang out as a woman came running into the center of the camp, blood pouring from a wound in her head. She screamed, "Washichun!" the Lakota word for "white man." The others in the tribe were shocked. The injured woman dropped to the ground, dead.

Then, suddenly, a group of pirate-looking white men in ragged clothes, yielding knives and guns and other sorts of horrible weapons, invaded the camp. The scene was horrifying. The Indians put up a good fight, but the ex-convicts overpowered them. Soon, every one of the Indians, man, woman, and child, was dead, their bodies lying lifeless on the ground.

An elderly Indian man appeared before Ryan. The man spoke in his Native Lakota tongue, but Ryan understood, as he was not listening to the language but to the communication itself.

"Ryan, son of many sons, this is what happened to your people. You are one of us, as your great-grandmother was Lakota. Because greed for the golden mineral consumed these men, they were willing to take our bodies and release our souls. They did find what they were looking for, but they did not heed their relationship with the Earth and her children, the animals. These men were greedy in taking without returning anything to the one who gave them sustenance. Our people, the Lakota people, loved the Earth and her children, as we were children of hers too. The white man thinks of Earth as something to conquer and own. We see her as something powerful we give thanks to, for providing us with deer and buffalo, which give us meat to eat, hides to keep us warm during the long winters, and bones to make tools and weapons from. Taking without giving thanks and taking without acknowledgement make Mother Earth very angry. She will not be ignored. Since this day you have just witnessed, when I, too, the holy Medicine Man of my tribe was killed, I have vowed to never let the white man forget what happened. The trees, earth, sky, animals, all the way to the tiniest of insects have agreed to make sure our story is never forgotten, and we have placed a curse upon any full-blooded white man who steps foot in these woods until the truth is told."

In the background behind the wise man, Ryan saw log cabins being erected, the white men cheering over the finding of gold, all fast-forwarding through time. But then he saw the forest consuming the men, animals killing them, the earth devouring them, something pulling them into the sky, the buildings being consumed entirely, leaving no trace of their existence. The Medicine Man continued talking.

"We were waiting for you, because by your words, you can tell the truth and set us free. We are sorry about the loss of your friends, but please trust that they are fine and that you will see them once again, in another time. Now is the time to tell the world the truth and to bring balance and harmony once again to this naturally peaceful forest. Now go and tell the truth."

The Indian and the visions disappeared from Ryan's view, but the same deer that had appeared to Adrianne appeared to Ryan. He followed it, and it led him out of the woods to his car.

***

Over the next week, Ryan completed his thesis, writing the truth of what happened, along with supportive facts from the local historical society, like the documentation of area tribes speaking of the "mysteriously disappearing Lakota tribe." Some who read Ryan's thesis disbelieved what he had to say, but the truth was now out there. Some history books even printed what Ryan had written, debunking the prior view. Because of the exposure of truth, the forest could be at peace once again. From that day forward, people of all races enjoyed its beauty and history. Ryan even lobbied for a memorial to be placed there with a plaque about the history of the Lakota and their views of the world.

Ryan believes that the night sky is a little brighter now because the souls of the massacred Lakota were able to escape their tragedy and ascend to the heavens as stars, to light the night sky for their descendents.

The Indian Boy

By Ava Wrightsman

This is the story of the Indian boy. It is a legend which grew out of the time, many years ago, when the white man moved onto the land that the Native Americans called home. The legend begins when the Indian boy was only six. He was out collecting sticks and wood for his mother when everyone in his small tribe was killed by a group of white raiders. He was spared because he was in the forest when it happened.

When he returned to the teepee, he found nothing but blood and death. His mother lay by the fire outside. Her eyes stared blankly into the sky. The boy had nowhere to go and no one to live with. His entire tribe had disappeared.

He went back into the nearby forest and cried tears of great sadness. While he called upon the spirits of his ancestors for guidance, the white raiders returned to his home and burned everything in sight. He was left with nothing but the clothes on his back and the jingling necklace his father had given him on his sixth birthday. It was a leather cord with shells, silver and turquoise strung alternately. Each object represented one of the boy's ancestors. The last two were for his mother and father. He never took it off.

***

Ten years later, a white man and his wife drove their covered wagon across the spot of land where the boy's tribe had lived. When the couple stopped to feed and water their horses, they heard a jingling sound. "I have the feeling we're being watched," the wife said.

"Oh come now, Agnes," the husband said. "What could be watching us?"

"I don't know. But I feel like the eyes of the devil are boring through the back of my head," Agnes said.

"Nonsense. You're just tired from our long journey. It's only another half day of travel until we get to our destination," the husband replied.

"I don't think we should stay here," Agnes said.

"Hush," the husband replied.

The jingling noise stopped and Agnes began to think that she had imagined the whole thing. But I think we all know that it was real.

The Indian boy was now sixteen. He crouched in the bushes nearby, watching these two white folk. He wondered what he should do. After all, it was white folk who had killed all his people. Would he be right to murder these two innocent white people? Or would he be going against the laws of nature and disrespecting the honor of his ancestors by harming them?

He didn't know. And he hadn't been taught much, since his family had been killed when he was only six.

The sun drifted down in the sky and the moon glowed above. Agnes and her husband went to sleep in the wagon.

The Indian boy had grown up among the animals for most of his life. He could move through the bushes with the stealthy grace of a mountain lion and attack ferociously with an old flint knife, using it like the fangs of a wolf.

When the white man and his woman went to sleep for the night, the Indian boy walked up to their wagon. He held his necklace still against his heart, praying that his ancestors would guide him. He climbed into the wagon and crouched above the white woman. Her eyes were closed. He touched her. Her face was soft.

She reminded him of his mother, when he'd found her dead by the fire. And then the woman's eyes fluttered open. The boy brought his face closer to hers. Her eyes were a soft color like the sky on a warm summer day. But then her face went white as the moon and she made a terrible sound—like a pack of coyotes baying over their latest kill.

The blood rushed through the boy's veins. His heart thumped in his chest. He tasted terror.

The husband grabbed his gun.

The boy ran from the wagon. He was swift. He was stealthy. But he couldn't outrun the gun shot that hit him in the back.

He fell in the dirt. His body lay lifeless on the spot where he had found his mother ten years before.

***

People say that the spirit of the boy never left. His ancestors inhabit the nearby trees, but the boy is doomed to roam the earth until he makes peace with the white man. Or until he gets revenge for his tribe. No one knows for certain.

***

150 YEARS LATER:

Boy Scout Troop 55 is sitting around the campfire. They're surrounded by trees that are said to be inhabited by Indian souls. They eat s'mores and tell campfire stories. Someone even tells the story of the Indian boy who lost his life in this very spot.

Then the scoutmaster, James, says it's time to go to sleep. All the boys climb into their sleeping bags. But one boy, Scott, is afraid. He's heard too many ghost stories on his many camping trips. And he hates to sleep under a full moon.

When Scott hears the soft snoring of his other troop members, he climbs out of his sleeping bag. He pulls on his jacket and tiptoes quietly through the camp to his scoutmaster's tent. He taps on the outside flap. James pokes his head out. He isn't surprised to see Scott kneeling down in front of his tent.

They've been camping together before. "Hey big guy, what do you need?" James asks.

"I, uh, I have to go to the bathroom and everybody else is asleep," Scott says. He has to think fast. He needs an excuse to be up in the middle of the night. Even though James probably knows the boy is afraid, Scott doesn't want to admit it.

"I did tell you boys not to go alone, didn't I?" James says.

Scott nods.

"All right. Give me just a minute and I'll slip on some shoes so we can go together."

A few minutes later, the scoutmaster and the boy walk toward the bathroom together. "Do you believe that Indian story?" Scott asks. There's concern in his voice.

"Nah," James says. "You know we just tell those stories to entertain you guys." He ruffles Scott's hair with his hand.

But then Scott hears a jingling sound. "Did you hear that?" he asks.

James stops walking. He shines his flashlight into the nearby bushes. "It was nothing," James says. "We've probably just heard that story too many times."

They take another step toward the bathrooms. They hear the jingling sound again. Only this time, it's closer.

They stop walking.

James turns around. He sees nothing.

Scott looks up at his scoutmaster with terror in his eyes.

"It's just the wind in the trees," James says. But he isn't so sure.

They turn around and take another step forward.

The jingling sound is so close, Scott is certain someone is right behind him. He turns around and the scream catches in his throat. He is facing a teenage Indian boy. The boy has a leather cord around his neck that holds shells, silver and turquoise.

The Indian boy takes a step closer. The necklace jingles again.

Scott is terrified. His breaths come in rapid succession. He doesn't know what is going to happen to him.

The Indian boy holds out his hand. He puts his finger on Scott's heart.

Scott is sure the ghost is going to zap his soul right out of his skin. He doesn't want to see his own death, so he closes his eyes.

But instead of a quick, cold death, Scott feels warmth fill his body. The Indian boy shares his courage with Scott, who feels strength spread out from his heart all the way to the tips of his fingers and toes.

For the first time in his life, Scott is certain he can face a ghost. In fact, he feels certain he can face anything right now. He opens his eyes.

The ghost is gone.

"Wait! Don't go!" Scott calls out.

The wind blows through the tall trees in the dark night. The moon shines high above. The Indian boy made peace with the white man.

Casper and Basper
By Ray Peck

The 2nd grade class sat around the campfire. They were very young to be out in the woods, but it was a special outing and some of the parents had come along, too.

"Tell us a ghost story!" one of the children shouted.

"Yes, yes!" the other children chimed in.

"Ghost stories can be scary," the second-grade teacher, Miss Holt, warned.

"I don't want to hear scary stories!" Rebecca said and nestled up next to her best friend Brenda.

"I do!" yelled Bobby.

"Yes, yes, please tell one!" several others joined in.

The teacher thought for a moment and smiled. "I know one I can tell you."

Rebecca covered her ears and squeezed her eyelids together.

"Don't worry, Becky. It's not *too* scary," the teacher smiled. The six-year-old cracked opened her eyes and looked carefully at the teacher.

Miss Holt looked over the class. "You know about Casper the ghost, right?"

"The Friendly Ghost!" several shouted.

"Well, I bet you didn't know that Casper had a baby brother?"

The class, and especially several girls, looked up with interest.

"His name was Basper."

***

"One day Casper went camping, just like we are today," Miss Holt began. "Basper came along. Remember, he was just a baby. They had a tent, right next to a large oak tree whose branches spread out across the sky above them. Casper brought Basper's crib and put it in the tent. Basper had just started to crawl, and Casper didn't want him getting into any trouble in the forest. The woods can be a scary place!

"Casper went away to check out the woods. He liked trying to find animals. He was a ghost, so he could fly through the trees and very quietly sneak up on them. He found some squirrels, a little family of rabbits, and even a deer!

"When Casper came back, he went into the tent to tell Basper about the animals he'd seen.

"The crib was closed but Basper wasn't there!

"Casper flew all over the campsite. But there was no Basper!

"He looked on the right side of the tree. He looked on the left side of the tree. He looked behind the tree. There was no Basper!

"There was nothing else around! Casper flew all around the edges of the campsite. There were no other trees anywhere close, just some way down the side of the hill. And he knew Basper couldn't go *that* far! He could barely crawl! There was nowhere else he could have gone.

"'Basper! Basper!' Casper called. Where was Basper? This was not good. His baby brother was gone! Did somebody steal him? Casper was very scared!

"Then Casper heard a faint giggling.

"He raced back and forth through the air as fast as he could. Then he stopped, listening to the soft laughter of the little baby's voice. It was coming from the tree!

"Casper went back to the tree and searched all the way around it, twice. He stared at it, and then put his head against the trunk. There was the soft voice of his baby brother.

"Basper was *in* the tree!

"'Basper!' he cried.

"Basper crawled forward until his little white head stuck out from the bottom of the tree. Since he was a ghost, he could crawl *through* things! He had been in the tree the whole time!

"Casper raced over to him, pulled him out, and they hugged and laughed. Casper then tickled him and Basper giggled and squirmed.

"When he put Basper down, the baby looked up at him in a funny way and suddenly floated upward! Casper couldn't believe his eyes. Basper had just learned to crawl through things and now was taking his first ghost steps. For a ghost, that meant flying!

"Basper rose up, little by little, until he was above Casper's head and kept rising. His arms were spread and he looked one way, then the other, then back again.

"Casper floated up and turned around so he was upside down, flying right underneath Basper, who now had the biggest grin anyone ever saw across his baby face.

"They laughed and hugged, high up in the air. They floated that way for a long time before coming down.

Many years later, both Casper and Basper thought it was the best camping trip they'd ever been on!"

***

"I like that ghost story!" Rebecca exclaimed with a big smile on her face.

"Aw, that wasn't scary," Bobby said.

One of the fathers slipped behind Bobby and shouted, "BOO!"

Bobby jumped.

Everyone laughed, including Bobby.

After everyone quieted down, Bobby asked, "Can I hear more about Basper?"

Seven-Leg Sam

By Catrina Worth

I met Sam many years ago, on a family camping trip. Dad and Mom had taken Marie with them to pick up a few things at the store in town, while I stayed behind to work on my insect and spider collections. To keep peace in the family, I was busily emptying out my nets into vials—outside of our tents.

I was especially proud of having found a fuzzy jumping spider, whom I named Sam. He was so furry, he looked almost like a teddy bear with extra eyes and legs. I knew these little guys could jump a foot or more, which came in handy for hunting down prey. All spiders don't spin webs, you see, and the jumping spider is one of those. They use a strand to secure themselves for long jumps, so that if they miss, they can crawl back up that strand. They lurk in ambush for their prey, or they chase them down; fast little things. Sam was particularly cute. I couldn't help smiling every time I looked at him.

By nightfall, I had secured all my vials and carefully put my field notebook, nets, and other gear away—in the trunk of the car. Mom, Dad and Marie were already sitting around the camp fire, juggling plates of barbequed chicken, potato salad and coleslaw in their laps. I joined them, telling them all about Sam, whom I was more excited about than I was about dinner.

Oddly, as I was talking about Sam, I thought I felt him run into my pocket. I freaked a bit, knowing that jumping spiders can give a nasty bite, and immediately pulled my pocket open, but there was nothing inside. I shrugged it off. Then it happened again. I looked again; my pocket was empty. *Hmmm. Could have been any insect*, I thought. But by the time we had roasted marshmallows and put out the fire, I had felt him more than a dozen times! Yet every time I looked for him, he was nowhere to be seen.

Marie and I kissed Mom and Dad goodnight, then climbed into our own tent and sleeping bags. "Can you leave the light on tonight, Jimmy?" Marie asked, meaning our lantern.

"Sure, Sis," I assured her, "I'm right here, though. There's nothing to be afraid of."

Just then Marie pointed at my pocket, eyes saucer-wide, "Jimmy, something is crawling around inside your pocket!"

Again?! I opened my pocket… to see absolutely nothing. "There's nothing there," I offered, but Marie wasn't buying it. "It's a ghost-spider, Jimmy!"

That struck my funny bone so badly I had to really hide the laughter. I didn't want her to feel bad, but—a ghost-spider?

"Well, if you see it again, you let me know, okay?"

She nodded, but shied away from hugging her big brother, which was a first. She clung to her stuffed moose, and didn't look like she would be falling asleep any time soon.

Having read Marie her bedtime stories at home since she was a baby, I didn't need the books to tell them to her. By the time I had finished "Thumbelina" and "The Little Mermaid," she was fast asleep. I think those stories put Sam to sleep, too, because he certainly was in our tent, as I discovered with the morning's first light.

I awoke, dreaming of Sam crawling around on my shirt. *Oh, not again!* I thought. *Well, a good shower will take care of this! Or maybe I just got too close to some poison ivy. Mom should have packed the zinc lotion. That should handle it if the shower doesn't.*

I unzipped my sleeping bag, and threw it off of me. Just then, Marie sat up with a start, eyes saucer-wide again. "Jimmy, it's the ghost-spider."

By this time, I was ready to accept any idea, even that of a ghost-spider. More importantly, when I saw the fear in Marie's eyes, I realized I had to be calm for the both of us. I immediately went into "big-brother mode." "Where do you see him, Marie?"

"He's right there, on the corner of your pocket." My calmness seemed to be spreading. She got out of her sleeping bag, and stood in front of me, where I was sitting on the edge of my cot. "He's right there," she whispered, pointing to my pajama shirt pocket. This time, to my amazement, when I looked at my pajama pocket, I saw Sam looking back at me with those two large, frontal eyes.

"Well, I'll be darned," I said softly, not wanting to disturb him. I was afraid a strong breath would blow him off of my pj's. "Hello, Sam."

"Hello, Jimmy," he answered. "Hello, Marie. Can the two of you help me find my back-right leg?" Concurrently, my mouth dropped open, my eyes blinked several times and my head moved back away from him. I quickly recovered from the surprise, now fully intrigued. Sam had spoken!

"Your leg?!" I asked in awe. "But I saw you had all your legs yesterday when I put you in the vial. Speaking of which, how did you get out of that vial? I put the lid on tight. You should be—" *Gee, how to break it to him?* "You should be dead in that vial, in my spider collection."

"I am!" he said, almost proudly.

"He's a ghost-spider," Marie reminded me.

I wondered if I was still dreaming. Then I realized that Sam's "mouth" had not moved when he spoke, yet I could understand everything he was thinking, as if he were talking. I decided that if this was a dream, it was a cool dream, and I intended to enjoy it!

Marie seemed to be interested in Sam, not frightened anymore. So I turned my attention back to Sam. "Say, Sam, how can you be dead in my spider collection if you're here with Marie and me?" I already knew the answer to that one before I asked it, but I had to hear it from his own "lips".

"That's not me in the vial, Jimmy. That's just my old jumping-spider body. Now I'm being a ghost-spider, which is lots of fun. I can run right through things—watch!" And with that, he ran through the wall of our tent, returning a moment later, laughing so hard that he almost fell over, despite having so many legs. "That was great! You should have seen it! There was a lizard outside, who ate me, but I just ran through his belly! He can't figure it out! Oh, it's fun being a ghost! You can have my old spider body for your collection, but I need my missing leg. Without it, I can't jump. I can still run, but I want to jump, too!"

"Well, let's see," I said, determined to help him, "Where do you last remember having your missing leg, Sam?"

He thought it over briefly, and seemed to brighten up. "I think I still had it when I was in your net."

"Let's check!" The three of us ran out to the trunk of the car. I found the net I had caught Sam in, and used a magnifying glass to carefully inspect it. Sure enough, there was one fuzzy jumping-spider leg caught in the net. I hadn't meant to tear it off when I had put him in the vial. I used a pair of tweezers to gently grasp the leg. Without having to ask Sam, I knew that the right thing to do was to glue the tiny leg to its body. A minute later, Sam's eighth leg was re-attached. I gently put the dead fuzzy jumping spider back into his vial.

I thought Sam would be sad at the sight, but instead, he heartily thanked me! Then he bounded from the trunk to my pajama pocket, where he stayed, while I carried Marie back to our tent. She seemed to be communicating with Sam, smiling, even chuckling from time to time. I sat her down on top of her sleeping bag, on her cot.

"Sam says he's happy now, Jimmy. He wants to run and jump and play… and by the way, he's ready to go outside to hunt down his breakfast, but he doesn't know how he'll keep anything he catches from falling through his ghost-body! He thinks that's very funny!"

I could tell she was right. I could "feel" great relief and laughter inside our tent. It seemed to grow and grow, as did a small, spider-sized glow. That glow grew bigger and bigger, as it floated to the top of our tent, until all at once, it exploded into a million pieces!

"Oh, no! Sam is gone!" Marie cried.

"No, I'm not, Marie! That's just one of the fun things I can do! I'm going to hunt down some breakfast now! Can you pet me before I go?" She gave him a gentle stroke; so did I. Then he was gone—just disappeared. But for years after that, when we camped at that site, he joined us in our tent for fairy tales at bedtime. And he always liked to be stroked when we said "Goodnight."

Fish Lake

By Bud Hayes

I was eight years old when my father took my younger brother and me on a fishing vacation in southeastern Oregon. It was a great adventure, filled with wondrous discoveries and activities. We caught scorpions under rocks, found odd skeletons along the creek beds and saw all kinds of things that we still talk about today. That was the trip where we crossed paths with a large mountain lion and I witnessed the greatest lightning storm I'd ever seen, with bolts shooting down from the sky, branching out in forks and striking the hill tops all around us. But the best story of all was when we went to Fish Lake.

Fish Lake was average-looking at first glance, with greenish water, thick brush along the banks and an old worn-out boat dock. We rented a couple of those old weathered boats, piled the fishing gear inside and went out. We trolled with long, sparkling "Ford fenders" and we even tried our luck with "super dupers," which were the fancy lures with red and silver reflectors and a triple hooks on the ends, but we weren't having much luck. As we trolled around that lake, we came to realize that these were smart, native fish, not the dumb and docile ones that the fish hatchery dumps into the lakes once a year. Oh no, these were tough and smart fish. They fought hard and wrapped themselves around sunken logs or the outboard motor to break the line. After losing several fish, though, we learned how to react. Every time someone hooked a fish, the rest of us had to scramble and reel in our lines, lift the motor, pull in the fish stringer and make sure there was nothing the fish could get wrapped around. As I said, they were smart fish. One of the biggest trout I ever saw was pulled up to the surface, but we didn't have the net ready and he broke the line and escaped. Well, all of us felt bad about losing that fish.

Most of the time I found fishing boring—letting that line dangle in the water for so long that I'd forget what I was doing—but not on this day.

My little brother had finally hooked something. It was a really big fish and he was fighting it hard. Attempting to outsmart us, the fish swam under the boat, looking for something to wrap around or rub against to break the line. As my brother tried to reel him in, the fish dove down under the boat and we figured we'd lost him. But a moment later, we saw something moving up toward the surface and up into the air. As the fish sailed above us, he jerked his head to the side, throwing the hook right out of his mouth. With mouths agape, we knew we'd been outsmarted by another fish and watched helplessly as he disappeared underneath the boat.

"Did you see that?" my brother gasped.

Before I could open my mouth to speak, I heard a splash off the side of the boat and before my very eyes, the same fish tossed himself right into my lap! Although it was a task to catch him, we'd outsmarted him.

No one ever believed me when I told them, "Yeah, the fishing was so good at Fish Lake that they jump right into your boat."

You don't have to believe me either. Just ask my brother Bob, or better yet, take a boat out on Fish Lake sometime.

Hank's Tale

By Mitchell Esterman

Hank, dog tired after riding for a day and a half, picketed his faithful Pinto, Paint, and started a campfire. He opened his saddlebag and took out the last of his bacon and beans, threw 'em in the pan he carried just for the occasion and got things a-fryin'. He also took out the pot and got things a-brewin'. When supper was ready, he hunkered down by the fire and poured his'self a cup of what he called "cowboy coffee" and took a big strong swig. It was strong enough to take the hair off a coon and it tasted good. When he had his fill of bacon, beans and coffee, he leaned against an old oak tree stump and went to Sandman Land.

***

Hank abruptly awoke to a soft touch on his cheek. "Wha—huh? Who are you?"

"I'm Ahkhanna, daughter of his Lordship Ammon, Master of the Northern Desert."

Hank was looking at the most beautiful, olive-skinned, black-haired woman he'd ever seen. She wore a white silken gown that flowed straight to the ground, covering her richly appointed leather sandals. Her hair was adorned with a garland of flowers.

"Pardon me ma'am, but this don't look like the Mojave Desert and you sure don't look like no settler's daughter. How did I git here, ma'am?"

"Why, you must have fallen off of your horse and hit your head when I found you. Come with me and we will get you cleaned up. What are you called?" Ahkhanna asked.

"My name is Hank, ma'am."

"That name will never do. We'll call you 'Hankhammon.'"

Hank chortled as he looked into her onyx eyes. "Anything you say!"

***

Hank followed Ahkhanna into a large desert city where he was taken to a bathhouse, stripped by two male Ethiopian slaves, bathed in hot mineral water and doused with perfume. He was then given a white silk tunic with a blue sash. He was shaved and his hair was cut.

After Hank's makeover, he walked with Ahkhanna as she led him to a palace in the middle of the city. Hank, in all his days, had never seen luxury such as this. They approached what appeared to be a meeting room in the center of the palace, guarded by two more Ethiopian slaves, who bowed to Ahkhanna and let her pass.

"Wait here until I present you," Ahkhanna said.

As the minutes passed, Hank waited outside the room in sheer agitation.

***

Ahkhanna presented herself to His Lordship Ammon, Master of the Northern Desert. He was short and stout, but of good build, and his head was bald except for a long braid that extended down his back. His piercing opal eyes belied his apparent docility. "Good day, my father," she said.

"Good day, my daughter," his Lordship Ammon answered.

"Father, I have a great gift for you," Ahkhanna whispered in his ear. "I have found the one."

"Very well, my daughter, bring him in."

"Father, may I present to you Hankhammon," she said, making a gesture to Hank who stood just outside the door.

Hank entered and stood before His Lordship.

"My fondest pleasure to have you honor us," said Ammon. "I have been waiting for such a meeting."

"Well, thanks to you, Chief," Hank said awkwardly, unsure of how he was supposed to respond.

"My dear, make our guest comfortable," Ammon told Ahkhanna. "Spare nothing!"

"Thank you, Father. And with your blessing, we shall depart."

"Off with you then!" Ammon waved.

As they left the meeting room, Hank said to Ahkhanna, "I'm not sure what I've done to deserve this, but I'm sure gonna like it. What's next?"

"Next, we present you to the very best of our kingdom," she smiled.

***

That evening an official banquet was prepared and Hank was the guest of honor. He sat with Ahkhanna on his left and her father, His Lordship Ammon, Master of the Northern Desert, on his right.

After the feast was devoured, His Lordship rose and raised his hand for silence. "Our prayers have been answered," he announced. "May I present to you, Hankhammon, the purveyor of our destiny!"

A loud cheer rang out among the crowd.

Are they a'cheerin' me? Hank wondered in amazement.

His Lordship Ammon proclaimed, "Sound the trumpets so the entire land knows of our success!"

"Yes, Your Lordship," the Captain of the Guard barked in reply.

As the band of trumpets blared, the room reverberated with more cheering.

Ahkhanna took Hank by the arm and led him through the town square where throngs of people were milling about.

Hank stopped to admire the construction of what looked like an elaborate religious altar, bedecked with beautiful tapestry, precious gems and trimmed with gold and silver that glinted in the morning sunlight.

"What is that?" he asked.

"That is the altar which is being prepared for the celebration, as we now have an appropriate sacrifice to the great God, Moloch," Ahkhanna answered, her onyx eyes sparkling as she smiled endearingly at Hank. "Come," she whispered, "let me take you to your room, so you can prepare yourself for the celebration."

***

Hank stood at the entryway of one of the most beautifully appointed rooms he'd ever seen. There was a gold and silver inlaid table with matching chairs, silk tapestry hanging from the walls, an ornate carpet covering the floor and a large feather bed.

My, oh my! This is purdier than the honeymoon suite at the Wichita Hotel!

Ahkhanna spoke softly, "Rest well until the festivities begin."

"Ma'am?" Hank asked. "What if I wish to go out for a while on my own?"

"Oh, I'm afraid that is forbidden," she answered, pointing to the two large guards with long, curved swords standing at either side of the entryway. "I will see you in a few hours to escort you to the festivities," Ahkhanna said before quietly slipping away.

Anxiety began to mount in the pit of Hank's stomach.

What is this place? he wondered, slowly pacing back and forth across the thick rug; back and forth, back and forth, the pressure building until he wanted to scream.

When Hank could take it no more, he moved to the door and spoke to the guard on the right. "Why am I being treated like this?"

"Don't you know?" the guard asked with a puzzled expression. "You are the Honored One who is to be sacrificed to the great God, Moloch!"

"What! Let me out!" Hank screamed, attempting to rush out the door. He was immediately stopped by the pair of guards as they made a cross with their swords, blocking the entryway.

Hank ducked under the swords and made a dash for the hallway. He felt the pain in his left arm as one of the guards grabbed it with a strength Hank had never known before. Panic coursed through his body and sweat began to bead on his forehead. He pulled back his right arm and landed a solid punch on one of the guard's noses. He heard a bone break; he saw blood spattered in all directions.

Gathering his senses, Hank bolted down the hallway, barely missing the groping hands of the other guard. Faster and faster he ran, feeling his heart palpitate until he feared it might burst.

Which way to go? The left? No! The right? No! Straight? Okay!

Hank saw it just ahead—a passage leading out into the open desert. He ran and ran across the sands until he could finally run no more.

Whew! Made it!

Hank looked around. There was no one in sight. Relieved for a moment, he began to walk as he tried to catch his ragged breath.

But where do I go? Where am I headin'? Which direction…

Hank stopped in his tracks.

What was that?

The clinking sound like rattling chains tinkled from behind. Slowly, Hank turned around and found himself facing a buffalo-hide shield and before he knew it, four guards grabbed him. He was unable to move, try as he might. He was helpless against their strength.

Gently but firmly, Hank was carried back to the room in the desert palace which now had become his prison.

Hank needed to get his bearings. He looked up to see four dressing maids waiting to prepare him for the ceremony and a throng of armed guards outside the door. Resisting no more, Hank knew that there was no way out.

***

Ever so slowly, Hank was taken from his room and promenaded through the courtyard as the crowd of onlookers watched in silence. As he descended down the steps of the palace to the main hall, the guards led him toward the altar of Moloch.

The cheers of the masses went up as one unison unified chant, "Moloch! Moloch!"

The god would soon be appeased.

Hank was taken to the altar and gently placed upon it by eight muscular guards.

Heart racing, stomach churning, and fighting against the leather bands that secured him to the altar, Hank resigned himself to his fate.

At least I'll die with mah' boots off, he thought.

There was silence as the High Priest slowly approached the altar of Moloch. He was followed by his lovely assistant, Ahkhanna, and in his hand he bore a razor sharp, jewel-studded dagger.

Hank's eyes were darting back and forth, looking for a last moment's reprieve.

The High Priest slowly raised the dagger while sending a prayer into the firmament, "Oh Moloch, Great Moloch, we present this sacrifice to you, so that thy craving will be appeased and thou will bring peace and plentitude to our land and our people."

In equal motion, Ahkhanna's soft, wet lips touched Hank's cheek as he felt the razor-sharp blade of the dagger touch his heart…

***

"What the…huh! Who…?"

Hank suddenly woke as his horse licked his beard-stubbled cheek with her tongue.

"Git away from here you varmint!" Hank hollered, swatting her away as he rolled off the bramble bush that was sticking him right in the heart.

Looking up at his horse, Hank sighed, "That's the last time I drink a cup of straight cowboy coffee and go for some shut-eye."

GONE

By Tomi Lyn Bowling

The horrific news of another child gone missing had consumed the villagers of Glenwood. Who was it this time and why does this keep happening? The story was the same every time; dark clouds would suddenly fill the crystal blue sky, huge winds so loud you couldn't help but cover your ears, suddenly whirled around, and there'd be so much debris blowing around that shutting your eyes was involuntary. Then, as suddenly as it came, the wind was gone, the clouds gone, and the sky would be crystal clear again, as though nothing ever happened. A strange silence and stillness is all that would remain. That silence was short lived as it would soon be broken by the heartbreaking screams of another mother, discovering her child has been the next to disappear.

Twenty nine children in less than six months, had disappeared. The event itself never lasted very long, the winds, the clouds, always exactly seven minutes. Every time, it was no longer, no shorter, just seven minutes of sheer terror for those trying to escape it. Some residents had given up all hope and moved away. Others refused to leave and continued in their relentless search for their missing children.

As a result of these mysterious disappearances, there has been an endless stream of restrictions and rules placed over the care of any children. No child was allowed outside to play except in a heavily guarded designated play area and only between the hours of 1:00 p.m. and 3:00 p.m. on Sundays. Schools were cancelled. No one attended church because the church was now home to some of the residents who no longer felt safe in their own homes out in the wilderness. Children were not allowed to walk to the store, fish in the river, walk to a friend's house or even take out the trash! They were quite literally prisoners in their own homes.

Stir crazy, Anita Thomas insisted she be allowed to at least take the dog for a short walk to the end of the family's fence, twenty five feet away from the house. Seeing how difficult the restrictions have been on the ten-year-old and hearing her heartbreaking plea for a few minutes of freedom, her mother reluctantly agreed to let her step outside briefly.

There were no signs of clouds, the winds were calm, and it was a dazzlingly beautiful day. "Surely it will be fine for just a few minutes," her mother said, as Anita bolted for the front door.

She was so excited that she nearly left without the dog, or the leash! She ran back in a gleeful explosion of happiness, grabbed the leash and cheered to the family dog "Come on Davey, let's go for a walk!"

Anita stopped about five feet away from the house and took a deep breath, holding out her arms and enjoying the sunshine caressing her face. While her hands were held up high she inadvertently let go of the leash and Davey ran off to enjoy his freedom. Anita turned her gaze downward to see where the family dog had gone. As her head turned, a mild, warm breeze came from the north and whisked her hair. Her mother had been watching carefully from the window. Seeing the breeze moving Anita's hair she flew out of the door, slamming the screen door open and shouting to Anita to get back in the house.

Anita was horrified and ran back into their house. She watched as her mother rounded up the dog and came back into the house. Anita did not realize what had happened and shouted at her mother for dragging her back into the house and interrupting her brief experience.

Just then it went very dark. Those ominous dark clouds appeared, the wind roared and the mother quickly bolted all of the windows and doors. She yelled out to her children, "hide in the basement!" The children, terrified, complied and closed the door behind them. Anita shook with fear and hugged her brothers and sister. She felt completely responsible and burst into tears realizing why her mother cut her trip short.

The mother hid behind the railings of the stairs while cowering on the steps so that she could see the door to the basement at all times. She grabbed the rifle she kept in the coat closet, loaded it, and waited. The windows rattled, the door shook, and the room became darker with every passing second. It was so dark all that the mother could make out was an outline of the basement door. The mother, trembling, let a couple of tears fall from her face and quickly wiped them with her forearm.

The seven minutes passed, the wind subsided, the sky cleared and the dazzling beauty of the day returned. The mother opened the door to the basement and yelled down to her children, "come up now, it's safe, it's over." She sighed from relief that they survived another attack, began checking windows and doors, listening carefully for any screams coming from the neighbors. It was silent. Not a peep came from any of the neighbors, nor anywhere, not even from their own basement. It did seem highly unlikely to hear silence from four children, ever. Stunned by this eerie thought, she yelled out to her children again to come upstairs. She ran towards the basement, now shouting, ordering them to come out. There was no reply. There was no sound at all. She ran down the steps to the tiny basement and there was no one there. They were all gone.

She collapsed on the floor, from an indescribable emotional pain, and screamed in horror as her neighbors came running over. She cried, hysterically, as two of her next door neighbors scoured every inch of her house while another hugged and rocked her back and forth. The children were nowhere to be found. They had simply vanished, adding to the long list of missing children. The neighbors, most of whom had also lost a child or two, comforted her. It was tragically heart wrenching and a deeply sad sight. It was clear, to see the pain these people felt.

***

Jack Langdon, a bounty hunter, arrived on the 10:00 a.m. train. The village mayor had sent for him by wire three weeks ago. Jack had a reputation for finding the impossible and nothing seemed to scare him. He was the perfect man for the job. Jack was a big lumberjack kind of a guy, very tall and strong looking. He had huge leather boots, a scruffy beard, was in desperate need of a hair cut and chewed tobacco. He seemed like a big, dumb character but surprisingly, he was incredibly intelligent. His list of accomplishments was mind boggling.

It did not take long for the news of the four newest disappearances to reach the train station so Jack was informed right away.

He wasted no time getting a ride out to the Thomas's farmhouse. As soon as the house was in full view, as pointed out by the driver, he stopped, got out of the carriage and stood there looking pensively.

After a few minutes Jack turned to his driver and said "they're all fine." The driver's eyes lit up and he asked, sheepishly, how Jack came to this conclusion. Jack just stared out into the open and said "I can feel them, they're all fine, and they will all be home soon."

The driver was more than skeptical and now thought he must be driving a real nut case around in his carriage. He contemplated how everyone in the town would feel about such a statement and decided to keep it to himself.

***

Jack arrived at the house and Mrs. Thomas remained inconsolable. A neighbor offered him a cup of coffee. Jack thanked her but declined the offer and went straight for the basement.

As he walked around the house and headed for the basement he continued asking questions. Jack asked about each disappearance and wanted all of the details. He wrote everything down in a little pocket notebook. He especially wanted to know about the first disappearance and seemed keenly interested in that particular time. He asked about how the children were treated before that time; "Were there lots of rules and restrictions? Were the children given responsibility? Did they have much freedom?"

The already devastated parents took insult with his line of questioning and one of them said so aloud to Jack.

Jack quickly explained that asking any question sometimes results in an answer that is unwittingly a big clue. The parents seemed to understand and even though they still felt odd about it, they gladly gave up any information hoping for the opportunity to simply hug their own child again.

***

As villagers heard news of the arrival of Jack Langdon, the farmhouse became the site of a village meeting. The crowd grew larger and larger. Jack asked to have only one person be talking to him as he could not keep up with the barrage of questions being tossed at him at an alarming rate. He kept to conversation with the local mayor, who had lost his six year-old son very early on. The roar of voices got louder and louder and then they were quite suddenly silenced by the darkness, the clouds, the horrific winds, and then by the slamming of doors and bolting of windows - as all knew too well, what this meant. Women wept in anticipation of yet another child going missing. Seven long minutes came and went. The creepy silence ensued.

You could hear a pin drop even with over seventy people there in the little farmhouse. All listened carefully for any screams nearby. They heard nothing.

A few minutes had passed. The roar of many voices took over. They all cried out that this was the event they had been speaking of. The huge group was ushered over to the town hall so that all could fit easily and be found by anyone else in the town looking for them.

Upon arrival at the town hall there were indeed others waiting for them. One family had just arrived, who's fourteen year-old son had disappeared. The cries turned into pleas to Jack to find their children.

It was while they were all at the town hall that something completely bizarre happened. The sky went dark, yet again. The winds seemed even louder than before. The hall went dark. Many of people had huddled together, some just covering their ears, until it was over. As their arms unlocked and they let go they all looked around to see if anymore children had disappeared. To their astonishment no children were gone. They looked outside the windows to see if anyone was coming in from outside the town. No one came. Suddenly they realized that Jack Langdon, himself, was gone. The hunter became one of the missing. He was the first adult to disappear.

The families proceeded to retreat to their homes in complete dismay. No one knew what else they could do. They were all quite devastated by the mounting losses and unpredictability of these tragedies. This was the longest night ever. Scarcely a soul could sleep this night. They all just seemed to be "waiting".

***

The next day the sun was hidden behind some rain clouds. It rained and rained; no winds, just rain. The clouds suddenly parted and a rainbow appeared. At that exact same moment Jack and all of the children came bounding down

Wilder's Hill, named after Michael Wilder, an old recluse that had lived there over 100 years ago. As fate would have it, not one of the children remembered a thing, nor did Jack. Jack remembered right up to the point that he disappeared. He knew he was hired to find the children and find them he did. But he could not explain how, or where they were, or what happened during their absence.

The Outhouse

By Kelly Reno

You know that old outhouse sitting just beyond the campsite? The one that doesn't have a light bulb in it and hasn't had a fresh roll of toilet paper for almost two decades? There's a reason for its current state of disrepair. The truth is, the park maintenance staff refuse to go in it. In fact, they won't even go near it. Not after what happened in there.

Twenty years ago, a group of teenage girls were camping on this very spot and they'd been up late telling scary stories around the campfire. One of the girls was pretty spooked and begged her best friend to walk her to the outhouse because she was afraid to go into the woods alone. After some whispering and giggling amongst the other teenage girls, the plan was set.

It started out as a practical joke. After the girl went into the outhouse, her best friend went through with the plan to lock the unsuspecting girl inside. Using a shovel, the girl's best friend jammed it through the door handle on the outside then ran back to the campsite where she told the others about the success of the joke.

Minutes later, the girl in the outhouse tried to get out, but found that the door wouldn't budge. She banged on the walls, tried to crawl out through the top and kicked at the door, but it was no use. She was trapped.

Back at the campfire, the joke was soon forgotten and the topic of conversation turned to jucier things like clothes and boys. The girls forgot all about their friend who was locked in the outhouse and before long, they fell asleep.

They say that the light bulb in the outhouse must have burned out and the girl was trapped in the dark all night long. Surely she called out for help, but nobody heard her desperate cries.

No one knows exactly how she died, but they found her body in the outhouse the next morning, her fingernails bloodied and a mask of terror frozen on her face. Some say she scared herself to death and had a heart attack. Others claim she suffocated from lack of fresh air.

Nobody knows for sure what happened in that old outhouse, but the marks where she clawed at the walls with her fingernails are still there if you look closely.

They say that the girl appears as a terrifying ghost when the door of the outhouse is closed all the way. Some people claim that the door locks itself from the outside and that flashlights mysteriously burn out after just a few minutes in the outhouse. And then, when you're all alone in the dark, helplessly trapped inside, you can hear the ghost of the teenage girl laughing at you as she plays the same practical joke that took her life twenty years ago.

So, if you ever use that old outhouse, take a friend along with you—*a friend that you trust with your life.*

About the Authors

The Way to Happiness Outdoors Club would like to give an extra special thanks to all of the authors who contributed their stories to this anthology. The original tales in this book were submitted by authors who responded to our requests for stories.

Tomi Lyn Bowling is a Southern California real estate broker, mother of four and author of many published articles about real estate. "The Cellar" and "Gone" are her first published fiction works. She loves to write and is currently writing two novels.

Barbara Bowman was raised on a farm in Minnesota. She wrote her first screenplay in near- perfect format at the age of eight, even though she had never before seen a screenplay. She later earned an MA in Film from Syracuse University in New York. She now resides in Silver Lake, California, with her partner Devin and their toddler daughter Hayden. She loves being a mother and doing crafts, including her handmade "So Ugly They're Cute" dolls. Barbara aspires to be a working screenwriter and is currently writing the Sci-Fi thriller, *Those Who We Forgot* as well as a romantic comedy, *The Sweet Life*. Barbara contributed "The Truth Be Told,", "The Howling" and "The Old Man" to this anthology.

Joanna Celeste started writing at the age of seven and pursued it professionally at the age of fifteen. Now twenty-three, she writes part-time while working in her family business and is compiling her writings for publication. This story is her nineteenth published work; her poetry, articles and short stories have been published in such media as newspapers, live readings, magazines and anthologies. "The Legend of the Milky Way" is the first of four stories that comprise "The Milky Way Collection."

Frank Clark was born in 1954 in rural Trenton, Missouri. At twenty years of age he thumbed his way to Los Angeles and once there, decided to stay. He is now a contractor specializing in bathroom and kitchen surface restoration. His favorite authors are L. Ron Hubbard, Mark Twain, Charles Dickens and Larry McMurtry. He enjoys outdoor activities, which include fishing and target shooting. Frank is married and has a teenage daughter. Other family members are a Boston terrier, 2 cats and a cockatiel. Frank contributed, "The Dare" to this anthology.

Mitchell Esterman was born and raised in Los Angeles and currently resides there with his wife. "Hank's Tale" is Mitchell's first published story. He is working on an anthology of poems that cover just about everything, which he hopes to publish in the near future.

Kay Farkas was born in England and immigrated to Australia in 1968 with her family. After leaving Australia, Kay traveled around the world, making her way to Papua New Guinea and Malaysia aboard a tramp steamer. From there she traveled to Bali, Thailand, South Africa, England and then settled in Canada, where she married and had two children. Kay now lives in Southern California with her husband.

Bud Hayes, a third-generation Oregonian, moved to Los Angeles almost six years ago for career opportunities after owning and operating a construction business. Currently he works as a certified California Real Estate Inspection Association Inspector and is the president of the Los Angeles Mid Valley chapter. Bud has a varied history with outdoor activities, including working as a ski instructor at Mt. Bachelor in Bend, Oregon. He is a scuba diver, boating enthusiast and plays blues harmonica. Bud volunteers with The Way to Happiness Outdoor Club. Often he is found to have an overactive imagination, but is kept under control most of the time by his wonderful wife and their new baby son, Dylan.

Garett Martell is Canadian by birth, American by choice. He is an author and screenwriter. Garrett wrote and co-produced *Absent* with Left Over Films for the 2006 48 Hour Film Project which is currently traveling the festival circuits. Rather than sticking to one genre, Garett has followed where his interests have led him, writing several other feature-length screenplays in various genres and is currently in production on one of his own screenplays. Garett lives in Los Angeles with his wife, their young son and one very presuming cat. Garett's short story, "A Campfire Tale" is based on a true story.

Kat Martell has been, among other things, a camp counselor, a dancer, a nanny, a teacher, an actress, an art gallery manager, a salesperson, an artist's assistant, a singer, an executive, a business owner, and most recently a mom and wife—but she has always been a writer. An avid crafter and self-taught seamstress, Kat has published numerous poems and articles through the years. "Cabin in the Hollow" is her first published short story and is based on actual events. Kat lives in Los Angeles with her husband and son, where she now works as a freelance writer and is writing her first novel.

Rebecca L. Mate, author of "A Bear Story," was awarded Short Story Laureate by the National Authors Registry and was published in *Verses* magazine. Several of her other short stories have been published in small literary publications and short story anthologies. She received Honorable Mention in L. Ron Hubbard's Writers of the Future Contest. Her poetry has been published as well. Two of her screenplays were finalists in a family-script competition at a film festival and many of her articles have been published. She is currently writing a novel about the global holiday for the arts, International Art Day.

Barbara Oliver was an avid camper in her youth. "The Ghost Camper" is a true story based on one of Barbara's camping experiences. Today Barbara is a real estate investor and woodworker. She lives in Clearwater, Florida, with her husband, two daughters and three dogs.

Oliver E. O'Rourke is an avid outdoorsman and accomplished cage fighter. His fondest memories are of the days when he was employed as a costumed character at an Orlando theme park before losing his sense of smell in a freak accident at a pickle packaging plant. "Don't Read This Aloud" is his first published story. Oliver is currently writing a thesis about Pomeranian Pattern Baldness and hopes that his work will help to find a cure. He is also working on a memoir about his days as a bouncer at a roadhouse in Fairbanks, Alaska.

Ray Peck is a part-time freelance writer and poet. He has been published in magazines, newspapers and poetry publications. He has been writing since 1968. In addition to writing, he enjoys exploring the hills of Los Angeles with his three doggies (on and off trail). Ray contributed "Casper and Basper" to this anthology.

Lucy Quigley grew up scribbling bits of stories on scraps of paper, in journals, notebooks and in the margins of event programs. She lives and works in the Los Angeles area, where she is the Executive Vice President for Administration at an independent film production company. "The Back Road" is Lucy's first published story.

Kelly Reno is a professional novelist and screenwriter. She is the author of thirteen published books including the *Halloween* horror series by Berkeley, based on the *Halloween* movies. As an author of many genres, Kelly has written books on business, beauty and adult fiction. Kelly lives in Southern California where she is President of The Way to Happiness Outdoors Club. She contributed the stories, "Sleep With One Eye Open", "SNICKERS" and "The Outhouse". She lives in Los Angeles, California.

Corinne Simon-Duneau is a translator, a writer and a nomad. She has visited and lived in over 40 countries in Europe, Africa and Asia. She's currently writing a novel about France during the German occupation in the 1940s. She has written two novels and numerous poems and short stories in French. Her late husband, a writer, encouraged her to write in English. "The Mill" is her first published short story in English and he would be proud of her. Corinne lives in Los Angeles with her two cats, Ziggy and Domino. She has two step-children and one step-granddaughter.

Susan Stroh is a journalist, award-winning short story and screenwriter, biographer/memoirist, ghostwriter and coach, working out of Southern California. Founder of LEGACIES ALIVE, biographies and films about "Movers, Shakers and Givers," Susan's motto is: "Celebrate what's right with the world and the gifted people in it." In 2007, her biography, *From Immigrant to Innovator, the Vision, Work and Legacy of Adolf Schoepe,* found publication. *Dancing with Gravity* and *You're Right Already!* are amongst books slated to be published in 2008. Susan currently coaches several novelists and screenwriters and has enjoyed a ten-year collaboration with writer/editor/author Heide Boyden.

Bob Sullivan, founder of The Way to Happiness Outdoors Club, is an experienced outdoorsman who spent years fishing and hunting wild turkeys in the Missouri Ozarks. An outdoorsman in Missouri, where truth is sometimes more beguiling than fiction, had better have a few good stories up his sleeve if he plans on holding his own in gab sessions at the Cozy Corner Diner. Now living in California, Bob's favorite pastimes are fishing, playing drums and getting "The Way to Happiness" booklets out to others.

Dick Sullivan grew up in South America, where vampires and werewolves pursued him relentlessly along the hills and coastline of his small town in Peru. He never actually saw any of the creatures, but of course they moved quickly and remained at the periphery of his vision while he dashed from streetlight to streetlight as the years fled past. He is convinced they followed him to Georgia, which forms the setting for his short story. Still running fast, he currently lives in Sunland, California.

Elizabeth Sullivan started writing short stories a couple years ago, when she was stuck in her tiny travel trailer some distance from home, exhibiting at an art show. Having little space to do any other creative endeavor, she hauled out her laptop and wrote. Elizabeth is an internationally published artist (painter and sculptor). Elizabeth lives with four cats in Elgin, Texas in the cutest little granny house you ever saw, near her three grandsons, with whom she enjoys adventures in the great outdoors (mostly having to do with sticks, rocks and puddles). Elizabeth can hardly wait until they grow out of toddler-hood, so she can teach them art and writing.

Catrina Worth and her husband live in Florida with an abundance of pets, all outdoor animals, which include a solid white, feral cat, a three-foot black racer snake, several neighbors' cats, dozens of geckos, a blue jay, two squirrels and a twelve-foot alligator named "Boots" (who lives in a pond on county-owned property next door to their house). She writes to entertain, teach, inspire and uplift—and for the sheer delight of writing itself! Catrina is currently working on an educational book for teens and young adults.

Ava Wrightsman lives in Southern California with her husband, her daughter, two cats and a big, friendly dog. At the age of eleven, with the help of her fourth grade teacher, she published her first book, *The Giraffe Who Helped Someone and Got What He Always Wanted.* She contributed the story, "The Indian Boy" to this campfire anthology. Currently, she is hard at work on a romance novel set in late eighteenth- century England about a governess who finds love and family in a most unusual way.

Myron Wszelaki lives in Los Angeles. He is a building contactor by trade, but his passion lies in "artistic creation"—of all types, particularly stories, sculptures and inventions. "Redemption" is Myron's first published short story and he is currently working on a dramatic novel about the relevance God has to man and the universe.

Permissions

Cover Illustration, *The Campfire*. Reprinted by permission of Nico Photos. ©2008 Nico Photos.
Interior Illustrations, *Because It Tastes Good, Redemption, Sleep With One Eye Open, The Hunter, The Dare* and *Oh-tay-yah*. Reprinted by permission of Elizabeth C. Sullivan. ©2008 Elizabeth C. Sullivan.
Because It Tastes Good and *The Axe in the Woods*. Reprinted by permission of Dick Sullivan. ©2008 Dick Sullivan.
Redemption. Reprinted by permission of Myron Wszelaki. ©2008 Myron Wszelaki.
Sleep With One Eye Open, SNICKERS, Don't Read This Story Aloud and *The Outhouse*. Reprinted by permission of Kelly Reno. ©2008 Kelly Reno.
Night Gobblers. Reprinted by permission of Bob Sullivan. ©2008 Bob Sullivan.
The Dare. Reprinted by permission of Frank Clark. ©2008 Frank Clark.
Old Medicine Woman. Reprinted by permission of Elizabeth C. Sullivan. ©2008 Elizabeth C. Sullivan.
The Back Road. Reprinted by permission of Lucy Quigley. ©2008 Lucy Quigley.
Ghost Camper. Reprinted by permission of Barbara Oliver. ©2008 Barbara Oliver.
The Howling, The Old Man and *Truth Be Told*. Reprinted by permission of Barbara Bowman. ©2008 Barbara Bowman.
A Campfire Tale. Reprinted by permission of Garrett Martell. ©2008 Garrett Martell.
The Mill. Reprinted by permission of Corinne Simon-Duneau. ©2008 Corinne Simon-Duneau.
The Legend of the Milky Way. Reprinted by permission of Joanna Celeste. ©2008 Joanna Celeste.
Cabin in the Hollow. Reprinted by permission of Kat Martell. ©2008 Kat Martell.
The Cellar and *Gone*. Reprinted by permission of Tomi Lyn Bowling. ©2008 Tomi Lyn Bowling.
The Bear Story. Reprinted by permission of Rebecca Mate. ©2008 Rebecca Mate.
Eva's Phone Call. Reprinted by permission of Susan Stroh. ©2008 Susan Stroh.
A Crack in the Lake. Reprinted by permission of Kay Farkas. ©2008 Kay Farkas.
The Indian Boy. Reprinted by permission of Ava Wrightsman. ©2008 Ava Wrightsman.
Casper and Basper. Reprinted by permission of Ray Peck. ©2008 Ray Peck.
Seven Leg Sam. Reprinted by permission of Catrina Worth. ©2008 Catrina Worth.
Fish Lake. Reprinted by permission of Bud Hayes. ©2008 Bud Hayes.
Hank's Tale. Reprinted by permission of Mitchell Esterman. ©2008 Mitchell Esterman.
The Way to Happiness, is a trademark owned by L. Ron Hubbard Library in the USA and in other countries (trademark registrations issued and other registrations pending and is used with its permission. ©1981 L. Ron Hubbard.

The Axe in the Woods

By Dick Sullivan

SPECIAL BONUS STORY!

EVEN FROM A DISTANCE, in the light cast by the blazing logs, he could count the people around the campfire. A dozen kids, maybe more. A few grownups. Nothing to worry about. He just had to move quietly.

After all, he was a Hunter. Sort of.

He smiled. Sort of.

There was a full moon. He liked that, too. A silver wash fell over the forest, turning golden where it met the firelight. When he moved, as he did now, pockets of the night sky appeared above the canopy of the treetops. Like anyone else that evening, he couldn't help looking up, looking for the burning rocks. In these mountains meteorites ruled the darkness. They were legend. They fell singly or in clusters, sometimes in showers of such intensity that only a photograph, studied afterwards, could give a count of their numbers.

The chance of witnessing such a storm of burning rocks brought the park's limit of tourists onto the mountain every weekend, especially during the fall and winter. The rocks fell year round, but never with the kind of visibility provided by the later months. Every weekend SUVs emptied to unload people from all over the country, even the world, turning the park from near wilderness to a city of tents and folding tables and gas stoves and chatter, cell phones and radios and Frisbees and laptops.

During the day the campers behaved like campers anywhere, sleeping, cooking, hiking, reading, riding mountain bikes, keeping tabs on kids. As the sun dropped to the horizon, everything changed. Tripods and camera gear of all variety emerged from tents and vehicles. People set them up and fussed over them in clearings, on park benches, on nearby ledges jutting from the forest, from makeshift platforms: anywhere there might be an unhindered view of the sky. They put away the books and laptops and brought out folding chairs and cots, sweaters and knit caps, thermoses and ice chests. The more adventurous hiked out to find exceptional locations on remote areas of the mountain. Everyone quieted down.

People were there to see and record meteorites. By the time it was dark, they sat or stood wordlessly sipping coffee in the unseasonably warm night, summoning the onslaught, watching. Even the kids behaved, enthralled by parents behaving more like kids than the children themselves.

Meteorites had nothing to do with the hunter's presence on the mountain. He had been surprised to see the party of kids and adults gathered around the white Toyota Highlander march out of camp to the far end of the park, up against the west of the mountain, where visibility in the little gully was notoriously limited. Yet this pleased him. It removed his quarry and himself further from public view.

And so he stalked closer, keeping the trees between him and the circle of light cast by the campfire. At its rim beside a tall pine, he saw a low rock nicely concealed behind a growth of ferns. Soundlessly he came up on the rock and sat down, certain he was invisible. Moving the fern leaves ever so slightly he found he had a clear view of the group around the campfire. He could hear the cross currents of a dozen conversations. And there was the one he sought. Unmistakable. A little boy, standing while the rest of the kids sat.

The hunter ran his finger along the blade of his axe. A little dull, but it would do the job. It wasn't a big job that was required of the axe.

He listened and watched. A woman in a turquoise windbreaker was urging the children to quiet down.

"It's time," she was saying. "Please give me your attention. Marcus, you, too. David, Gloria. Thank you. Peter, won't you sit please?"

"No, I like to stand!"

The hunter felt the heft of the axe in his hands. The small boy talking was the one he was watching intently.

"Sit down, Peter!" echoed a half dozen voices.

"I'll stand if I want!"

"That's okay," the woman said. She knelt beside the little boy. "If you want to stand, you certainly can."

"Good, 'cause no one messes with me!"

"Big talker," a boy behind Peter said.

"I'll show you who's a big talker!" Peter spun around and put up his fists. He was hardly half the size of his challenger.

From his hiding place the hunter shook his head. He noticed a pair of older boys sitting in the back row of kids. One of them had his legs crossed and elbows propped on a backpack in front of him. In the firelight it seemed he was regarding Peter thoughtfully. The boy seemed familiar somehow, but the hunter couldn't place him.

"Peter and Marcus, no fighting tonight!" The woman stood and put her hands on her hips.

"Miss Tony, Peter's got attitude!" Marcus complained. Another half-dozen voices spoke up in agreement.

"That's enough, all of you," Miss Tony said. "Why are we here?"

"Campfire stories!" the kids answered.

"That's right. We've got this new book full of stories and we're going to read a whole bunch of campfire tales around the fire and when we're done, you're going to vote on the ones you like best. The ones that scare you the most or make you laugh the hardest, it doesn't matter which—"

"I'm not scared of any silly ghost story!" Peter said.

The hunter had to keep himself in check. He wanted to leap out and discipline this little boy, right now.

"It's not polite to interrupt, Peter," Miss Tony said. "Now you'll all get to vote on the stories you like the most. Three of our older kids have volunteered to take turns reading them. Paul, Cindy and Josh. We'll have plenty of marshmallows for roasting as we go along. And when we're done, we have a special surprise for everyone. Now, is everyone comfortable and ready to get started?"

"Oh, yes!"

"Scary stories!"

"Ghosts!"

"Vampires!

"Werewolves!"

"Marshmallows!"

Everyone laughed.

"I'm not scared of anything!" Peter again. But apparently tired of standing, he plopped down in front of Marcus, who gave him a shove with his foot. Peter turned around and hit Marcus on the leg.

"Why don't you behave?" a girl beside Marcus said.

Peter stuck his tongue out at her. He scooted forward out of the range of Marcus' foot.

"Let's have our first reader," Miss Tony said.

An older boy in a red plaid shirt stepped up. The campfire flames gave him plenty of light to read by.

"I'm ready, Miss Tony."

"Okay, Josh," Miss Tony said. She sat down between a pair of kids. They immediately snuggled up to her and she put an arm around each. "Then away we go."

The hunter watched from his hiding place. He had his plan now. He would wait a bit longer. Let them tell a few stories. Let the fire die down a bit. Let the tension build and the ghost stories work their spell. Let the moon go behind the mountain, throwing them all into shadow. Then the time would be right. He leaned back quietly against the tree beside the rock and made himself comfortable.

Through the ferns he could still make out the outline of the little boy named Peter, sitting apart from the rest of the kids. A troublemaker, that one. He settled the axe across his knees.

The boy in the plaid shirt began reading in a deep voice designed to add some drama.

There'll be plenty of drama tonight, the hunter thought. And he closed his eyes and listened to the campfire stories.

***

The campfire tales held the hunter spellbound and kept the axe idle in his hands. Vampires, werewolves, aliens, demons, avenging spirits and all the stuff of imagination left their pages in the book the children were reading and bit, tore, terrorized and enchanted their way into his mind. Just one more story, he told himself. And kept telling himself. The hours passed. The moon slid down on dark and invisible rails behind the mountain. Now there were just stars, legions of them, pulsating from galaxies without end. But all stories, and the books that hold them, do have an end, now, as in the time of the Arabian nights. The hunter realized he had heard the last of the campfire stories. There was a collective shiver from the children as the reader, a teenaged girl, spoke her final words and closed the book.

Cindy, the last reader, completed her story. For a moment there was no sound but the popping of embers from the fire.

"Creepy," one of the kids finally said.

"Really creepy," said another.

"They were all scary. I'm not going to sleep tonight," Rachel said, sitting next to Marcus.

"With one eye open maybe, like in that story!" said Marcus.

"I would never go into that old mill, not for a million dollars," Susan said. She leaned closer to Miss Tony.

Beside Susan, Andrew said, "Not for two million!"

"Ha! I wasn't scared at all," said Peter, getting his six-year old body to his feet. "Silly old stories. You guys are 'fraidy cats!"

"Not scared, even a little?" Miss Tony said, smiling.

"No way! I would beat up any of those vampires or werewolves. No ghost can get me! I'm too tough!"

The sky, empty now of the moon, had enclosed them in a dark vault the starlight couldn't penetrate. Only a faint amber glow stirred in the waning fire. One of the adults appeared with an armload of logs and arranged them on the red coals. Almost instantly, fresh yellow flames flickered up the sides of the logs.

"After all these campfire stories, a good fire is what we need," he said, laughing. "Keeps anything out in the woods away."

In the woods behind them, something wasn't going away. The hunter, in spite of himself, had joined the audience. Now that the tales were over, he began to prepare himself for the assault.

Brace yourself, my young Peter, he thought.

But before the hunter could move, Miss Tony stood.

"Now. We were going to vote on the best stories, right?" she said.

"Right!"

"The oozy thing from the lake!" Susan said.

"Aliens on the loose!" said Marcus.

Another kid yelled, "The old graveyard story!"

"The mountain lion and the turkey guy!"

"The old man in the cabin eating everybody! And the candy bar story!" from the back row.

"You must be hungry," someone said.

“’Fraidy cats!” Peter repeated.

Miss Tony put up her hands. The kids quieted down. “Well, before we vote, we have to hear all the stories, right?”

“But you said that was the last one,” Marcus said.

“I said the last one in our book. Remember what I said when we started? That we had a surprise?” She turned and looked behind her. “I’d like you all to meet Jordan. Jordan, come on over, please.”

From the shadows a taller boy uncrossed his legs, stood and walked over to Miss Tony. He dropped his backpack at his feet and brushed his hair from his eyes.

“Jordan is a special guest of ours,” Miss Tony said. “In fact, Jordan is why we are here tonight having so much fun. He’s involved in a program that I am very much in favor of, and together we came up with the idea of an evening of campfire stories. His will be the last story, and you get to vote on it, too.”

“You have a scary story?” Susan asked.

Jordan smiled. “I guess you’ll tell me.” Jordan looked about fifteen, maybe sixteen years old. The fire was starting to blaze again, outlining Jordan in a warm glow.

“I don’t need to read anything,” he said. “I know this story by heart.”

Mrs. Ogilvie’s Gift
By Jordan Cruz

I started out, same as you, new to this world. No one gave me a road map.

It seemed to me even when I was very young that I had two choices. I could do what everyone else told me to do, or I could do what I wanted to do. Maybe you’ve felt this way sometimes, too.

But I found out much later that really wasn’t the problem. The problem was that no one ever gave me a way to figure out what I should do. My parents tried, but as a kid I could never really listen to them. There were teachers, school counselors, older kids, and gang members, as you'll see. It seems I got orders, rules, and lots of 'you better do this!' But I never got shown how to figure things out on my own, so I could make my own way. Not in any way that really seemed like a truth that came from me. And by the time I learned, it was almost too late.

Almost.

Down the street there was this boy named Johnny Tillman. We used to play together, even before grade school. Johnny lived in a small one story house on this little bit of land between two large apartment houses that were full of gang members. Some really mean kids lived in those apartments. Johnny's mother and father, well, something happened to them when he was young. That little house between the apartments was his grandmother's house, and he came to live with her when he was four years old. They were really poor and Mrs. Ogilvie, Johnny's grandmother, had a reputation among the kids as a grumpy old woman. That first Christmas she gave Johnny a skateboard, and she would come out on the porch and watch over Johnny as he rode that board up and down the little sidewalk that connected her front door to the street, keeping an eye on him. And letting the gang members know he wasn't on his own, I guess.

That's the way I first met Johnny, him just riding that little skateboard up and down, up and down that sidewalk, for hours and hours, every day of the week, and always there was Mrs. Ogilvie watching him like a hawk. On weekends and during the summer I would skate down from up the street where I lived, and since Johnny wasn't allowed to leave that twenty foot stretch of sidewalk in front of his house, I would skate alongside him and for hours on end up and down, up and down that sidewalk we'd go.

For one whole summer and most of another, there wasn't a day I didn't spend some time riding with Johnny Tillman there in front of his house. Johnny never got tired of skating that little concrete patch. But I did. Some days I'd just have to say goodbye to that old sidewalk and skate away to visit some of my friends who lived in other neighborhoods. When I'd come back hours later there Johnny would be, still skating that sidewalk, the sun down behind the buildings and the streetlamps just flickering on. There too would be Mrs. Ogilvie, in the shadows of her porch, making sure Johnny never strayed, as if the world might swallow him up if he did.

Johnny was a couple of years younger than me, and it wasn't long before skateboards lost their hold on my imagination. As the years slipped by I started running with some older kids. One of them played the guitar in his own band, and started teaching me. I had a paper route for a while and saved my money and one day went down to this little corner music store and bought myself a guitar, and for a long time I studied playing that cheap guitar for all I was worth. Just as I started to get pretty good, my friend with the band moved away and the other kids I ran with started getting mixed up in some of the gangs in the neighborhood, and so did I.

I hadn't seen Johnny in a while, and one day I went over to his house. Mrs. Ogilvie came to the door and told me Johnny was off riding in the skateboard park.

"Why don't you go on over and say hello, Jordan," Mrs. Ogilvie said. "That boy gets up, skates for an hour before breakfast, goes to school, comes home and skates till dark and I have to drag him off to bed. In the morning it starts all over. He could use an old friend to break the routine."

"Sure, Mrs. Ogilvie," I said. But I wasn't interested in seeing Johnny, if all he was doing since he was four years old was riding that old skateboard. Secretly I felt it was time for him to grow up, and after she'd gone back inside I went and looked up my new friends in the apartment next door. I didn't pay any more attention to Johnny Tillman.

By the time I was ten years old, my guitar was stuffed somewhere up in the closet shelves and I was more interested in being tough and talking back to my parents and slipping out of the house after hours and hanging out at the park. I quit my paper route. And pretty soon I was in trouble.

I'd like to say nicer things about myself, but the truth is I got into some pretty big trouble. I didn't always get caught, but I was always in trouble. The second time I got suspended from school was the worst. One afternoon I was with some guys and I don't know what happened, but before I knew it we were all throwing rocks at the back of the school and breaking windows on the second floor. There were some girls inside one of the rooms and one of them got hurt pretty bad with broken glass falling everywhere. The next thing I knew there were policemen all around and they took me and this older kid down to the police station. A lot of the kids got away, but this older one, a real gang member, whispered to me, "We don't snitch on anyone."

I got put on probation that time, and because I wouldn't tell on any of the other kids who had thrown rocks with me, the gang elevated me to one of the top candidates to join as a full member, even though I was the youngest kid there. My parents didn't know what to do, and it had been years since I could talk to them anyway. All we did was yell at each other

One day I was coming home from school and there was Johnny Tillman skating toward me, a block or so away. As I watched he suddenly came off the ground, it seemed maybe three feet high, did a complete three-sixty turn and landed perfectly. I remember thinking, how did he do that? There was no ramp, no incline, no nothing. He just seemed to rise into the air, his feet glued to that skateboard. Then he did it again, only this time he spun a turn and a half and landed backward, rolling straight down the dead center of the sidewalk. Next he leapt a foot off his board, spun himself around and landed face forward again, back on the skateboard, his balance perfect. All this in about five seconds. I wasn't sure I had seen it, it happened so fast.

Johnny was only a few feet away before he recognized me. We hadn't seen each other in quite a while and I was, well, dressed differently these days. You know, baggy pants, baseball cap, earrings. Johnny still wore jeans and tennis shoes unraveling at the edges. His skinny arms still poked from an old faded tee shirt.

"Hey, Jordan," Johnny said, stopping that skateboard like it had brakes. I waited for him to say something about my probation, but he said, "Nice seeing you. Still playing guitar?"

"Nah," I said. "I get my music ready made. Are you still skateboarding?" I said it pretty nasty.

Johnny laughed. "Well, I guess so. Driving my poor grandmother nuts. Hey, come on over for a while. Have dinner with us, you can call home from our house. I got some birthday cake left over. I'm twelve years old and a day!"

Now, the truth was, my probation meant I had to be at home right after school. But I said, "Sorry. I got things to do. With my boys."

Johnny looked at me. He was a small kid still, his long brown hair making him look even younger. "Some other time, okay?"

"Yeah, why not?" I said, and walked away. In a few minutes I turned onto my street and walked toward the apartment houses where all my gang member friends lived. The truth was, I was starting to get nervous about some of the things they wanted me to do. And next week was supposed to be my initiation. Part of me was proud of being accepted, but another part was worried. Initiations could involve some pretty scary things.

I looked up and found myself looking at Mrs. Ogilvie, sitting on her porch, waiting, I supposed, for Johnny to come home to that little house of his sandwiched between the apartments. But I had just passed Johnny headed the other way, no doubt, on his way to the skateboard park.

Mrs. Ogilvie's hair was a little whiter than all those years ago when Johnny and I used to skate away the summer days on her narrow patch of sidewalk, her face lined with a few more wrinkles. I recognized the dress, though. That hadn't changed.

"Jordan Cruz," she said. I stopped in front of her house. Something in her voice told me I had to. From her porch chair, Mrs. Ogilvie lifted her wrinkles in a smile.

"You ever look at my poor old sidewalk? Really close?"

"I don't guess so," I said. "It's just some old concrete."

"Look at it now. Tell me what you notice."

I looked at it, not feeling I had much choice. It was an old habit to mind Mrs. Ogilvie.

"It's just an old sidewalk," I said again.

"You haven't looked, Jordan. Now really *look* at the sidewalk, won't you?"

So I did. And there was something about it. It wasn't—smooth, or flat, or something. More like it had little valleys all over it.

"Do you see them?" Mrs. Ogilvie said. "That boy of mine has worn grooves in that old concrete. I had to start letting him go down to the skate park just to have any sidewalk left at all."

It was true. That's what I was seeing. Up and down, up and down, years on end. Johnny would have ground that sidewalk into dust. And kept on going, I guess, all the way to China.

"Do you still play guitar, Jordan?" Mrs. Ogilvie asked.

The same thing Johnny had asked. This time, though, I had a memory. Me in my room, my fingers on that cheap guitar's neck. The hours passing. Feeling good about coaxing those chords to come out right, one after another. About how my fingers responded. Feeling music. Feeling alive. Feeling like—me.

"That guitar's up in the closet somewhere," I said. "I'm too busy these days to fool around with stuff like that."

Mrs. Ogilvie stood up. She walked down her porch steps and right up to where I stood. Not as quickly as she used to. In her hand was a little package of some kind, wrapped like a present. There was even a little bow on it.

"I've been wanting to give you this for some time," she said. "I think it's time."

Mrs. Ogilvie held the package out for me to take.

"Go on," she said. "It's for you."

I took it from her. It was a flimsy thing and bent in my hands.

"What is it?" I asked.

"It's for you, like I said," Mrs. Ogilvie answered. "I gave Johnny one just like it for his birthday years ago. I know he would like you to have this one." She put the back of her hand lightly on my cheek, letting it linger for just a moment.

"It's a little book, Jordan. A sort of road map. One day a long time ago I was riding the bus home from the hospital. It was the day after I lost my daughter and her husband, Johnny's parents. This young girl across the aisle must have noticed me. I'd been crying for days, it seems. Without any other word she said simply, 'This is for you.' And she gave me a handful of little books. 'One's for you,' she said, 'and the rest are for those you love, or anyone you'd like to help.' I didn't look at the booklets and I didn't tell her thank you. At the next bus stop she gave me a smile and got off. I do wish I could have thanked her. I looked for her all the years afterward that I rode the bus, but I never saw her again."

"What happened to Johnny's parents?" I asked.

Mrs. Ogilvie hesitated just a little before saying, "It was a car accident. The kind you hear about all the time. The kind that happens to everyone else's family."

"I'm sorry, Mrs. Ogilvie." I was, too.

"Those little books lay unread in one of my drawers for a long, long time, Jordan. A long foggy time. One day I realized Johnny was my boy now, and that same day I went and threw out all the liquor bottles in the house and opened that drawer up and took out one of the books. For some reason I had always remembered the title, and I wanted to see what a little book with a title like that had to say."

"What does it say, Mrs. Ogilvie?" I looked at my present, but somehow I didn't want to unwrap it.

"Well, that's for you to find out, Jordan, if you want to. That young woman told me to give a copy to those I love. You've always been special to me, and I was always grateful you spent so much time with Johnny when he was so young. Someday when you feel you don't have all the answers you need, the way I did those years ago, I hope you'll open it up and read it. And I hope it helps you as much as it did me."

Mrs. Ogilvie touched my cheek again and then turned and went back inside her house. In all the years I had known her that was the longest conversation we'd ever had. I went on home and as soon as I opened the door it was the same old thing: my mother yelling at me for being late, for leaving my clothes lying around—the same old stuff. I yelled back, went in my room and threw Mrs. Ogilvie's present up in my closet on the shelf with my guitar. I slammed the closet door, then went downstairs to yell at my Mom some more.

The days passed and one day a block or so from school, an arm shot out from behind a stone wall and nearly knocked me down.

"Yo, bro, whassup?" The voice was familiar, but not pleasant. "You never do know what's just around the corner, do you?

It was the gang member who was kind of assigned to me. He called himself Hero and I never knew him by any other name. He wasn't in school and I had no idea what he did all day. As a candidate for full membership in the gang I had to do the things he told me to. Already I had done some bad things. Shoplifting music CDs, dragging my house key along the side of expensive new cars, sneaking out of my room before daylight to bring him and other gang members coffee and donuts from the convenience store.

And there were drugs. Hero and other gang members did drugs in front of me, but said they would decide when I was ready before I could do drugs with them. When I had proven myself, they said. Until then, I could keep bringing them their coffee and donuts.

Now Hero said, "We vote on you and some other dudes Saturday night. Day after tomorrow. You know what? I'm gonna recommend you. But there's one last thing. C'mere."

Hero took me by the arm and led me from the sidewalk, onto someone's lawn. There was an old oak tree in the center of it and Hero walked me to it and pinned me against it with one hand on my chest, leaning on me hard. In his other hand he held a brown paper bag.

"This is it, dog. Your last test. Are you with the program?"

"Yeah, sure," I said.

"There's this kid you know. Scrawny little dude. Won't have nothin' to do with the boys. Too good for us. Thinks he's hot with the skateboard. You know that skinny little freak won some state championship or something, goin' to national games and even got some sponsor behind him. Dude's gonna be on television, man. They're payin' him hard money, man, for what? Stupid skateboardin', that's what. Ain't no way it's gonna happen. And that's where you come in."

A light was slowly turning on. "You mean Johnny Tillman? He's going to those big games next month? In Los Angeles?"

"Yeah, goin' out to California. You believe it?"

I didn't know what to say. In my mind I saw Johnny as a five year old kid, riding that skateboard back and forth on that same small stretch of sidewalk, grinding it away. And I saw his face. That earnest look he always had was concentration. The look of someone in training. At five years old.

"So here's the deal. You take this--" Hero handed me the bag he was carrying—"and you put it in his school locker in the morning. Dude never locks it. Then you take this--" he shoved something in my sweatshirt pocket—"and slip it under the principal's door when you're sure the old man's at his desk. And you run and get out before he can drag himself up to see who's there. You got it?"

"What's in the bag?" I asked. It was a small bag, but heavy.

"You can check it out at home, dog," Hero said. "I know you were tight with this kid at one time. That's why we chose you. Let's see if you're ready to soar with the eagles. You don't do this, I can't recommend you, dog. You see how it is?"

"Yeah, I see."

"We'll see, then." Hero gave me a smirk inside that hard look of his. He dropped his hand from my chest, and I could breathe again. He turned and walked across the lawn, then stopped at the sidewalk and looked back at me with another twisted smile. "Don't be doing any jaywalking while you're carrying that bag. You don't even want to get stopped by the cops on the way home."

Hero pulled his hood up and put his hands in his pockets and shuffled away. It was a long five blocks home and it seemed forever before I finally opened the front door and went straight upstairs to my room. I hadn't looked in the bag, but I had a good idea by now what was in it. I don't know why, I just did. I sat there for a while before I opened the bag and looked inside.

It was a gun. A revolver. I took it out and put it on the bed beside me. Pieces of shiny yellow metal, like golden dimes, stuck out of the back of the silver wheel and I could see the dull orange tips of the bullets inside.

There was a plastic sandwich wrapper in the bag. It was partly full of a brown crushed plant. I knew what that was. I dropped the wrapper back inside the bag. I looked at the gun for a long time. Then I put it back in the bag, too.

I remembered Hero had put something in my pocket. I unfolded the piece of paper, and read what it said. I read it twice, then let it fall to the floor. I got up and went and sat by the window, resting my arms on the sill, the way I used to when I was really young, just to enjoy watching the world outside and imagining all the wonderful things in it.

But mainly I thought of Johnny Tillman.

The sun was dropping below the industrial buildings on the horizon when I left the window and opened the closet and got Mrs. Ogilvie's book out, still in its gift wrapping. I sat on the bed next to the paper bag with the gun and the drugs in it. I wondered if the day came for everyone when they would have to choose the road they would travel. For me the two roads were obvious: the paper bag or Mrs. Ogilvie's gift.

I slid down and sat on the floor, my back against the bed. I removed the gift wrapping carefully and looked at the thin little book an unknown young woman had once handed Mrs. Ogilvie, who would one day hand it to me.

The booklet had a simple cover, mostly white. A little blue trail wound off into the distance toward a yellow sun. I smiled because I couldn't help seeing Johnny Tillman skating along that trail, up and down, up and down, before disappearing into a golden sunset.

Or dawn.

I was glad I had hours before my parents would be home, and I started reading.

***

"That's it?" asked Marcus.

All eyes were on Jordan as he sat down by the edge of the campfire. "Pretty much," he said.

"But what did you do?" asked Susan, pushing herself up from Miss Tony's lap.

"I straightened up and started flying right," said Jordan. "When I read the book I knew exactly what I had to do. About the drugs, about gangs, about school, about life. I saw where my life had gone wrong. I knew what I really wanted and I knew if I worked at it I could have it. And I saw it wasn't a contest between what others wanted me to do and what I wanted to do. It was just a matter of doing what was right. And the book showed me how."

"But what did you do?" insisted Susan.

"I fixed my life the best I could. I talked things over with my parents and they helped me. I went back on my paper route and paid for things I had stolen and for cars I had damaged. I quit the gang forever. I went to school and made it mean something. I took that guitar down from the closet and started playing again. I have my own band now, and we just recorded our first CD." Jordan reached down and picked up his backpack. "And because you're all very important to me, I have a gift for you. The same one Mrs. Ogilvie gave me." He paused. "I could use some help in passing it out."

The boy who had been sitting beside Jordan stood up. He was tall and skinny. He was obviously an older boy, but something about him made him look like the youngest kid there. He walked over and said with a big grin, "I could give you a hand."

Marcus blurted out, "I know you! Your pictures are all over the skate park and the board shop. You're the guy who won the skateboard games in California last month! Last year, too! You did stuff no one's ever seen before!"

"Meet my friend Johnny Tillman," Jordan said.

Marcus applauded enthusiastically and the other kids joined in politely.

Johnny bowed. "Thank you, guys. I'm here because I really want you to have this book. My grandmother raised me on it. She read it to me at night like a bedtime story. Before I was five years old I knew what I had to do to reach my goals."

Jordan took out a handful of the booklets and he and Johnny began passing them out. As Johnny got to Peter, the little boy suddenly sprang to his feet. "But I can't read yet! How do I get to reach my goals?"

"Why, you just get your parents to help," Johnny said. "Your Mom or Dad can read to you."

"They never read to me! They're always too busy!"

"Well, you just ask them to," Johnny said.

But Peter stuck his lower lip out and plopped down again, staring at the fire darkly. "I'll never reach my goals," he said.

In the woods behind the campfire the hunter listened to Peter's complaint in disbelief. A shock wave of recognition ran through him. The axe in his hand felt ridiculous. His carefully chosen beat-up old clothes felt foolish. His life suddenly felt ridiculous and foolish.

Sheepishly he got up from his rock and walked toward the campfire. As he stepped into the light the kids all gave him a funny look. Miss Tony stood up and stared at him.

"Mr. Hunter?" she said.

"Dad!" Peter jumped up again. "What are you doing here? Your clothes are all torn up. I'm telling Mom!"

Gerald Hunter shook his head. He tossed the blunt axe on the ground beside him. He couldn't help smiling.

"Hello, Miss Tony. Hi, Peter. I guess I should explain. I got this big idea, just after Peter left to come up here, that I haven't been a very good Dad lately. Like Peter said, I've been too busy. And not just lately, but all my life. All Peter's life. Knowing you were going to be telling campfire stories, my big idea was to dress up and, well, maybe give everyone a little scare. Maybe bond a little bit with my boy. Impress him with my cleverness."

"Don't tell me," Miss Tony said. "An axe murderer." She laughed. "You forgot to pour ketchup all over yourself."

Hunter reached behind him and pulled out a bottle full of the red sauce. "I just never got to that stage."

"Hello, Mr. Hunter," Jordan said.

Hunter looked at him and in the better light of the fire recognition dawned.

"Well, we meet again. From the bushes I did think you looked familiar," he said.

"I hope your car paint is holding up, sir."

Hunter laughed. "It got fixed fine, Jordan. Don't you worry about it. I still enjoy telling people about the day you knocked on my door to pay for the scratches you put in my car two years ago."

Hunter knelt down beside Peter. "Son, here's what we're going to do. We're going to do as much reading together as you want. And from what I've heard tonight, I think I need what's in that little book you've got as much as anyone else here. What do you say we make an agreement? When we get home, we'll read that book together. A little each night until we're done. And see what happens."

"We can reach our goals!" Peter said.

"Are we going to vote on the best story?" asked Susan.

"Look!" Marcus jumped up and began stabbing his finger overhead. "Look!"

Everyone looked. Above the silhouette of the treetops orange and yellow streaks flooded the night sky. The burning rocks came in a rush of tiny white-hot brushstrokes dabbing color on a black canvas, criss-crossing, chasing each other, nearly colliding, careening in a dance of light. Everywhere on the mountain shutters clicked, camcorders whirred, images formed. Then the meteorites vanished.

"Like seeing dolphins in an open sea," someone said. "They're there, they're gone."

"I like your story best," Peter said to Jordan.

***

The book that Jordan read was called *The Way to Happiness*, a common sense guide to making good choices in life.

If you'd like to read the booklet, visit The Way to Happiness Outdoors Club web site at www.TWTHOC.org and click on, DOWNLOAD A FREE E-BOOK on the side menu where you may download and read a copy for yourself.

The Way to Happiness Outdoors Club is part of a non-profit organization of dedicated volunteers that puts on family outdoor sporting activities to raise funds to print and distribute copies of *The Way to Happiness.* Since the formation of our club in 2003, we have distributed over one million copies worldwide.

You're invited to contact us at our website. We'd love to include you among our members and see you on one of our upcoming adventures!

The Editors